Forgotten Love

Firehouse Blues Series: Book 9

AE Moran

The Invisible Publishing Company

Firehouse Blues Series

Contents

Chapter 1: Jessie

The fire alarm blares through Howe Firehouse. The deafening noise echoes off the walls so everyone on the fire crew hears it.

I rush to the rescue truck and scramble into the back with Sophie McNish. Keith Brewer and Billy Cates ride up front with Keith taking the wheel.

Caleb Watts, Ellis Barrett, and Danny Brewer ride in the middle seat in front of me and Sophie.

"We got a ruptured gas main under the paper plant!" Billy reads from the dispatch notes on the computer. "Some of the building walls are unstable. Dispatch is unclear if any patients are in danger or how many."

"Why are so many gas mains rupturing all of a sudden?" Danny asks.

"Maybe we got a gremlin in town," Caleb tells him.

We don't talk the rest of the way to the scene except to talk about our equipment.

"A paper plant isn't likely to pose an air quality risk," Caleb points out. "We probably won't need our SCBAs."

None of us knows what to expect when Keith parks the truck across the plant parking lot. We get out to meet the plant managers.

Forty people stand off to one side. "At least thirty more people are still inside and unaccounted for," a tall female manager tells us. "We don't know where they are or even if they're in danger. We didn't want to go back inside."

Four engineers show up from the city gas company. "We shut the gas off. The plant should be safe."

"Take your SCBAs just in case," Duke tells us. "You don't have to put them on unless you smell gas."

He divides us into teams. I go with Caleb, Ellis, Danny, and Billy to one side of the plant.

The lady manager explains the situation to us on the way. "A few explosions went off under the building and some of the walls collapsed. They blocked off sections of the plant. We had to evacuate before we went back in to check if everyone got out okay."

"So the gas and explosions didn't cause a fire inside the building?" Danny asks.

"No, we never saw any fire. We heard explosions and felt them coming through the floor. Then we smelled gas and we all got out. That's it. The plant general manager did a head count of everyone who made it out, but we don't know where the others are or what happened to them."

Danny nods and pauses at the entrance. "Go back with the others," he tells her. "We'll take it from here." He casts a flinty gaze around at the crew and nods. "Let's go."

He pushes open the doors and we walk into the plant. We walk down a bunch of corridors searching every room. We come to the big main plant floor. All the machines stand still and silent.

We search that, too, and don't find anything. We go upstairs and search dozens of offices. We make it halfway across the plant before we meet Keith, Carter Holt, Theo Gough, Vince Jaeger, and Josh Barrett coming from the other direction.

"I still don't see any sign of unstable walls or explosions," Danny points out. "Everything looks intact."

"Go back the way you came and check any areas you haven't already checked," Keith tells him. "If we still don't find anything, we'll touch base with Duke and see what he wants to do."

We head all the way back in the opposite direction. We cover most of the same territory we've already covered.

Danny is just getting ready to tell us to leave the plant when we come to a maintenance block we didn't know about before.

We walk in and find ten men in blue overalls lying all over the floor. Broken concrete blocks lay scattered nearby from one of the walls that has fallen in.

We spread out to check the patients, but I'm the only paramedic here.

I do the quickest possible assessment on all of them. "We need to transport all of them," I tell Danny. "Any walking wounded would have gotten themselves out already. All these guys are critical. We can't do anything for them down here—not with the gear we have."

Danny checks the surrounding building structure. "You stay here with Ellis. Caleb and I will go back up to the vehicles and bring down as much extrication equipment as we can carry. We'll bring back a bunch of our guys to help load these people up." He regards me. "Will you be all right on your own?"

I nod and bend back over the nearest patient. "We'll be fine. You go ahead."

Caleb, Danny, and Billy leave. I start an IV on one patient and give him a shot of epinephrine.

Then I move over to another and put him on oxygen, but I can't help them all. I can't do half the things I know I need to do to all of them.

I find an old man lying near the back wall of the room. His pulse is weak and he seems to be breathing just fine. I don't see any injuries on him.

He's the only patient in the room who is awake with his eyes open. He gasps for air and his wild eyes dart around the room before he sees me.

"Help me!" he chokes. "Help me!"

"What seems to be the problem, Sir?" I ask. "Can you breathe? You don't seem to be injured."

"My inhaler!" he wheezes. "I need....my inhaler....."

"Where is it?" I pat down his pockets, but I don't find anything.

He raises one shaky hand to point across the room. "In my locker .....Jorgensen...."

I turn around. "Ellis! Get into that locker over there and find this guy's asthma inhaler. His name is Jorgensen."

Ellis must have been listening to our conversation because he does it instantly. He tears open Mr. Jorgensen's locker and comes over with the inhaler.

"Help me sit him up," I tell Ellis and take hold of one of the patient's arms.

Without warning, Ellis says in a clear voice, "We need to get the patients out of this room, Jessie. That wall is going to collapse."

His eyes shoot to the wall behind me—the same wall I was planning to lean my patient against.

My head snaps up fast and I stare at Ellis. This is the most he has spoken to me since John Brewer's death. It's the most Ellis has spoken to anyone.

I don't have time to make a big deal about him actually talking to me. I glance up at the wall and see dust sprinkling from some cracks running through the concrete surface.

Leaning my patient against it might have caused the whole wall to crumble. It would have crushed all of us and probably killed half the other patients in the room and me along with them.

I glance the other way. Mr. Jorgensen is the only conscious patient in here.

"Take his arm and we'll drag him outside," Ellis tells me. "Then we'll get the others."

I bend my head and grit my teeth to do it. I don't know how much time we have left.

It must have taken a lot for Ellis to tell me this. He must see something that makes him certain the wall is unstable.

We both take hold of Mr. Jorgensen's arms, drag him outside, and prop him against a different wall across the corridor out of danger.

I kneel down next to him to help him use his inhaler while Ellis goes back into the room.

He starts dragging patients out of there, starting with those closest to the wall. He pulls out three of the biggest men by the time I finish with Mr. Jorgensen.

I go back inside to help Ellis. We pull out three more people.

We're on our way back in for the last three. I walk in first with Ellis behind me.

I bend over to assess the first patient when Ellis tackles me from behind, grabs me around the waist, and yanks me back through the door just as the wall collapses into the room.

Rock, rubble, and concrete slabs tumble across the floor and dust blocks the room. Ellis scrambles to get off me in time, and right then, the rest of the crew shows up.

I give them the quickest explanation possible. Keith, Danny, Ellis, Billy, and Caleb go back inside and extricate the last three trapped employees.

I get busy helping Josh, Carter, Sophie, and the other paramedics stabilize the patients who are already in the corridor.

We don't get a chance to talk before we deliver all the patients to the hospital. I'm just leaving the Emergency Department when Fire Chief Duke Broebeck comes around a corner and spots me.

"Are you okay?" he asks me. "Danny says you and Ellis got caught in a cave-in."

"We didn't get caught in a cave-in because Ellis pulled me out and saved my life. He saved all our lives, Duke. We all would have got trapped in that room when it collapsed."

He frowns at me. "What did he do?"

"He told me the wall was unstable and that we had to get the patients out of the room." I shake my head. "You could have knocked me over with a feather. He said it so clearly—like he used to before John's death."

"Wow," he exclaims. "I didn't know he still had it in him."

"Then he pulled me out of the way when the wall came down. I don't know what's wrong with him, but he's still got it."

"Do you think he would have said anything if the other guys had been with you?"

"I don't see why not. Ellis has always been a dedicated firefighter. He wouldn't keep information like that to himself just because other people might hear him talking. I don't think this has anything to do with people hearing him talk."

Duke studies me extra closely. "I wondered if he did it because it was you."

I find myself blushing. "I don't think so. He would have done the same thing for anyone on the crew. He's as dedicated and selfless as he always was."

Duke nods. "Head back to the firehouse. I'll need to get a full statement from you for the incident report, but that can wait."

I go back out to the ambulance and ride to the firehouse with Drew Killian and Chris Daniels. They've been transporting patients since we arrived at the paper plant scene.

The crew spends the rest of the shift restocking all the vehicles, giving Duke statements about what happened, and checking our gear.

I return to the rescue truck to find everyone from the call standing around talking.

"Did Duke rake you over the coals yet?" Caleb asks.

I laugh at him. "He didn't tie me to a chair and beat me up with a garden hose if that's what you mean. I just had to tell him what happened." I pull my SCBA out of the truck and stand it on the floor.

"What are you doing?" Sophie asks.

"I want to check the tank and regulator valve to make sure they didn't get damaged when I fell."

"Fell where?" Danny asks. "When did you fall?"

"You, Billy, Caleb were outside. You weren't there." I glance over my shoulder toward the other side of the garage.

Ellis stands over there checking his own SCBA for any damage.

Ellis and I were always close before John's death. Some might say we were sweet on each other, but neither of us ever acted on it.

Maybe our friendship and working relationship was too important for either of us to jeopardize it, but I always liked him and he always liked me even if we never became a couple.

I'm the one who has tried the hardest to bring him out of his self-imposed silence. He never listens and I've given up long since. What's the point in trying?

Could today mark the beginning of him coming out of it?

"What's wrong, Jessie?" Sophie asks. "Is there anything wrong with your apparatus?"

Ellis doesn't look up to notice me watching him. I watch him from a distance a lot and he never notices.

I turn back to my friends. "It's fine. I was just thinking about Ellis. He talked to me during the call. He warned me the wall was going to collapse and he was right. He even told me what to do to get as many people out as we could."

"Wow, really?!" Chris exclaims. "That's amazing! I didn't think he would ever talk again."

"He always talks when it's a matter of patient or crew safety," Josh points out. "He never says much. He always keeps it as short as possible, but he never keeps essential information to himself. He cares too much about the job."

"I don't think he'll ever go completely silent," Carter adds. "It isn't like he lost the ability to talk. He's just withdrawn. He's still in there. He's still the same person he was in every way that counts."

I find myself looking at Ellis across the garage floor again. "I sure hope you're right. Maybe this is the start of something. Maybe this is the first crack that will bring him out of this."

"I wouldn't hold my breath if I was you," Keith tells me. "Whatever is wrong with him won't go away just because some patients were in danger."

I sigh and heft my SCBA back inside the truck. Just then, Ellis finishes checking his apparatus.

I brace myself for the moment when he brings his gear to the truck at the same time, but he doesn't. He takes his apparatus to the stairs and carries it upstairs to Duke's office.

Chapter 2: Jessie

I knock on Duke's office door and he looks up from what he's doing. "Hey! Come on in," he tells me.

He leans back in his chair and waits while I shut the door behind me and sit down opposite him.

"How you doing?" he asks. "How do you feel about how everything is going?"

I shrug. "I guess I feel pretty good about it. I can't complain."

"How are you feeling about everything since John's death? How do you think it affected you and how well do you think you're bouncing back from it?"

I squirm in my seat and try to look away, but Duke has a way of commanding attention from anyone.

"You know....I'm not happy about it," I reply. "He was a great guy and he made the firehouse what it is. Things will never be the same without him.....but in a way, things are the same without him because you're here. I guess we all just have to keep going and doing the job, so that will never change."

"How do you think his death affected you personally?"

"Besides all the upheaval and drama of you coming to work here? I don't think his death affected me much at all. I was just really worried about all my friends—and I'm still worried about whether Ellen and

Oakleigh are going to be okay. I was worried at first that the firehouse would be okay, but then you started taking over."

"So you don't worry about that anymore?"

"No. You seem to be as competent as John was."

He smiles at me and blushes. "Thank you. I'm glad to hear you say that. Are you ready to get started with your performance evaluation?"

"I guess so....if I really have to."

He laughs and does something on his computer. "I don't have anything to say about your performance overall. Your attitude, execution, and skill have always been top-notch. I couldn't ask for better. You're an asset to this crew—but you already knew that."

I try not to grin. "Does that mean I can go?"

"Not so fast. We need to talk about your professional development."

"What about it?"

"Your next development tier is training for certification as an advanced paramedic. It's the next step to you becoming a paramedic practitioner."

I try not to stiffen. "I don't want to train to become an advanced paramedic."

He looks up. "Why not?"

"Because there aren't any positions open at Howe Firehouse for advanced paramedics. Advanced paramedics work on rescue helicopters, Coast Guard ships, and in hospitals. I don't want to leave the firehouse."

He leans back in his chair to study me. "So you have no desire to advance your career at all?"

"Not really."

"Do you plan to spend the rest of your career in frontline emergency work?"

"Is there a problem with that? I'm happy where I am. I don't want to leave."

"What would you say if I told you that you could get certified as an advanced paramedic and still work here?"

"I would say you were either lying or misinformed. Advanced paramedics command a higher salary than regular paramedics. The department couldn't keep me on as an advanced paramedic—and we don't have access to the medications I would be certified to use as an advanced paramedic anyway. It wouldn't make sense for me to go through the training if I wasn't going to use it."

"Most people want to go through the training precisely so they can level up their careers. They want the higher salary, the safer working conditions, and the more stable work hours."

"I don't want any of that. I want to stay here."

He takes a minute before he builds up the nerve to say the next part. "I wouldn't normally say something like this to one employee about another, but it seems appropriate for this situation. You may remember that the State Health and Safety Commission offered the Fire Chief position to Keith Brewer before they offered it to me. He turned them down because he didn't want to take John's place."

"Yeah? What does that have to do with me?"

"John left notes in Keith's file recommending him for professional development and leadership training so he could train to become a Fire Chief or even a captain. John made that recommendation while he was still alive. He had no way of knowing that Keith would be thrust into the role when Andy shot John."

I frown at him. "I still don't see how this pertains to me getting certified as an advanced paramedic."

"I'm getting to that. When I told Keith about John's recommendation, Keith didn't want to do the training because he also didn't want to leave the firehouse. He thought gaining the skills and training to be a Fire Chief meant he would have to move away from the people he considers family."

I nod. "I can understand that."

"I told him he should get the training anyway because he might need to use it. Something might happen. He has a family to support...or something might happen to me and he would have to step into the role anyway. Him getting the training would be what's best for him, his family, and the firehouse—and it turned out that I was right. He took over when Naomi and I got trapped in those tunnels—and he took over again when Amelia's mother surrendered the baby to us and I got stuck here taking care of her."

I don't know what to say. I see where he's going with this.

"I think you should get the training whether you leave the firehouse or not," he goes on. "What you do with the training or where you work isn't really relevant. You should advance your medical training either way. You don't know when you might have to use it—and your circumstances might change. Then you might wish that you had it—and I wouldn't be doing my job if I didn't push you to advance your career. I don't want you to stagnate."

I shrug at nothing. "Okay. I see your point. I guess I could do it."

"Great. I'll sign you up for the course and you can get started. Was there anything you wanted to say or ask me before we wrap this up?"

I open my mouth and stop myself. Then I look away. "I guess not."

"Is something on your mind?"

"You asked how John's death affected me."

He looks up at me. "Yeah?"

I hesitate again and then blurt out, "It's Ellis. There must be some way we can get through to him."

Duke leans back in his chair again. "I know you care about him and you want to help him."

"Of course I do. I can't stand to see him suffering over this for no reason. Even Carter has tried to talk to him."

"When I first came to work here, everyone's attitude toward Ellis made me worry about him, too. I spent a lot of time watching him and trying to come up with ways to ease the transition for him."

"Can't you send him for counseling or grief therapy or something?" I ask. "There must be some service for firefighters dealing with grief and trauma."

"There is. There are tons of services for us, but they're all voluntary. I couldn't order him to go unless it was affecting his job performance."

"It is affecting his job performance," I counter. "He's a completely different person than he was before."

"He's a completely different person, but it hasn't changed his job performance at all—unless you believe some of the people on this crew who think he's even better now than he was before. Some people say he's more motivated, more helpful, more energetic, and more attentive. Would you agree with that?"

I look away again. I don't want to think about that.

"I know you've been keeping an eye on Ellis, but you aren't the only one," he goes on. "I've been keeping very close tabs on him to make sure his performance doesn't fall off, but it doesn't. His behavior doesn't affect how much the crew respects and trusts him, either. His behavior seems to be having the opposite effect on everyone around him. It seems to bring everyone closer to him."

I don't know what to say.

"Would you agree with that?" he asks. "Do you respect Ellis less or trust him less now than you did before?"

"No! Not at all."

"Do you think his silence is in any way detrimental to crew cohesion or patient care?"

"No. So you won't do anything?"

"I can't do anything. If it was affecting his performance or his standing on the crew, I could compel him to go to counselling or grief therapy, but that isn't the case. I appreciate that his personality and behavior are changing, but if you look at it from a different perspective, an outside observer could be forgiven for thinking he's changing for the better."

I gasp out loud. "How can you even say that?! You don't know what he was like before! He was a great guy! He was funny and talkative and lively."

He glances at his computer. "His records also indicate that he was rather immature. Some of his early performance evaluations state that he had trouble taking the job seriously. He joked at inappropriate times in ways that made his crewmates, patients, and other emergency workers uncomfortable. He was known as a joker and not a serious professional. He's none of those things now. He is a serious professional. He's more professional and dedicated now than he ever has b een."

I cringe. Duke is absolutely right about Ellis.

"You have to realize that I am the outside observer here," Duke goes on. "I know you care about him and watching him completely change into a different person must be hard for you, but I have to evaluate him based on certain job performance metrics. How funny, lively, and talkative he is doesn't enter the equation. You're too attached to the person he was before. From what I can see, this new version of him isn't any less than he was before. He's still a great guy. He's just different."

I squirm in my seat.

"Was there anything else you wanted to say to me? Are we in agreement about this?"

I can't stop fidgeting. "I guess so."

"You can go, then. Feel free to bring up any other issues you have. My door is always open."

I leave his office feeling worse than when I went into it. I would almost rather have Duke give me a bad performance review than to hear that there's no way to help Ellis.

I've been going crazy about him. He won't listen to anyone, not even Carter.

Like something out of a bad dream, I run into Keith and Danny as they come up the stairs on their way to the breakroom.

"Did you get fired?" Keith teases and immediately scowls when he sees my expression. "What's wrong, sweetie? Don't tell me Duke gave you a bad performance evaluation. I'll never believe that."

"I just....we were talking about Ellis again. Could you guys talk to him? He needs to know that you don't hold him responsible for John's death—and I'm sure Ellen doesn't, either."

"We've already told him a million times," Danny chimes in. "So has Ellen and Carter has already thanked Ellis many times for saving his life. If Ellis doesn't listen, telling him again won't change anything."

"There must be something we can do! We can't just leave him like this."

"What do you think we should do—that we haven't already tried?" Danny asks.

Keith comes over to me, rests his hand on my shoulder, and peers deep into my eyes. "I think we all need to start accepting that Ellis will probably be like this from now on. I know you probably don't want to hear it, sweetheart, but you can't keep driving yourself crazy about this. You have to let go of the person he was and just accept him and appreciate him for the person he is now."

He gives me a deep hug and pushes me back. "Keith is right," Danny adds. "Ellis is still a great guy—one of the best. He's a member of our crew and we all respect him. I can't give him any higher praise than that."

Keith is right. I don't want to hear it, but I don't want to argue about it, either.

I can't let go of the person Ellis was before. I loved him the way he was before. He was one of my best friends. He was the sweetest guy who ever lived.

Now I don't even know who or what he is. He's a stranger to me now.

It's worse because I can't even talk to him to get to know him. He pushes everyone away, but it somehow hurts me so much more than it hurts anyone else. I was closer to him than they were.

Chapter 3: Ellis

I take my duffel bag out of my locker, stuff in my extra uniforms from my last few overnight shifts, and take out a bunch of dirty socks from the bottom of the locker.

I have the next two days off from work, so I'll be doing laundry when I get home.

I zip up my duffel bag, shut my locker, and turn away to leave the firehouse. I'm off shift now.

Danny Brewer, Josh Abbott, and Carter Holt all clap me on the shoulder, tell me I did a great job today, and wish me a good weekend.

I do my best to smile at them all, but I can't connect to them the way I know I should. An invisible barrier separates me from all of them—especially Carter.

He's one of the crew members who has tried the hardest to bring me back into the fold since John's death.

Everyone says I shouldn't blame myself for John getting shot. Carter would be dead now if I didn't get to him in time.

I wouldn't want to trade Carter for John. I don't even know why I hold my distance from the crew.

I just can't stop thinking about that day. The whole sequence plays out over and over in front of my eyes.

I even relive the sensations of my body flying through the air, colliding with Carter, and both of us hitting the ground.

Then I go through the same sinking agony when I see John lying on the ground with half his head blown off.

I guess that's what this is all about. I can't snap myself out of it. John is dead.

I worshiped the ground the man walked on. I don't even know what the world means anymore without him here.

Don't get me wrong. I admire Duke Broebeck. Duke is a great Fire Chief. I can't stay anything against him. He just isn't John.

I guess I feel like I'll be dishonoring John's memory or something if I stop thinking about him and remembering him.

I know that isn't true. Keith and Danny are moving on with their lives. They're even enjoying their lives. They have to. Keith has a baby son and Danny has a stepson and one of his own on the way.

If Keith and Danny can move on, I should be able to move on, too. I don't know why I'm doing this, but I don't seem to be able to stop.

I go through the same sequence of thoughts every damn day that I come in here to work. I can't stop thinking about it, dwelling on it, and nagging at it.

I wish I could stop—even for a little while.

I head out of the firehouse and turn into the parking lot heading for my pickup. I put my duffel bag into the bed and pull out my keys to unlock the driver's door when someone calls out to me. "Ellis—wait!"

I don't have to turn around to know who it is. Jessie Nash has never stopped trying to talk to me ever since John died.

I turn around very slowly as she comes up behind me, but I don't look at her. I can't look at her. I can't look at any of them, but she's the worst.

I care about her too much. That's the worst part in all of this. I hate that my behavior hurts her so much.

I wish I could help her—or at least stop hurting her. I wish I could break out of this if only for her sake.

I don't have to look at her to see the pinched expression of concern in her sparkling black eyes.

I used to love to see her pointed, elfish features light up when I joked around and made her laugh. She still smiles and laughs just as beautifully as ever, but never at me.

She always frowns in concern whenever she sees me. I'm a problem for her.

"I just want to say....thank you....for what you did on that call earlier," she stammers. "I know it's hard for you to talk to people....and I'm really grateful. You're a hero."

I don't say anything. I stare at the ground while I imagine her wincing that I can be so heartlessly cruel to her.

She's six inches shorter than I am. Wild, springy energy winds up her petite, wiry body. She usually wears her witchy black hair in a ponytail when she's on the job.

Now she's taken out her air tie to let her hair hang loose. I used to love the way she looked. Now everything about her hurts. Just being around her hurts because I know how much she worries about me.

"We're having another barbecue at the beach tomorrow," she tells me. "You should come. I know you have the day off, but it's been so long since we saw you at a barbecue when you weren't rostered on duty. What do you say?"

I shrug at nothing. I won't go to the barbecue. My presence will only upset people, especially her.

I can't let myself get involved with anyone from the crew. Seeing Ellen and Oakleigh would be a nightmare. It's bad enough I have to see them when I'm rostered on barbecue days.

I wish I could do something to make it up to them, especially Oakleigh. She has a right to get depressed over John's death.

So does Ellen, but she pulls it together to take care of her step-daughter. Ellen only took a few weeks off from work before she went back to her job as a paramedic at the hospital.

Jessie shuffles her feet in front of me a few more times. It always goes like this whenever she tries to talk to me. I shouldn't have talked to her at all on that call, but I had to let her know that she and the patients were in danger.

Me talking to her about that only gives her false hope that I might come out of this. I don't know how I can or if I can or if I even should.

Is this what my life is going to become—a living monument to a man who's already dead?

She takes a step forward and squeezes my arm. "Anyway…we would love to see you there if you want to come. Thank you again. I'm really grateful for your help."

She walks away. Thank God. All the rest of the crew has given up trying to talk me down from the window ledge so to speak.

I wish she would do the same thing. I wish she would stop worrying about me—but I can't stop worrying about myself. I guess that's the problem.

She goes back inside the firehouse. I get in my truck and drive away. Now I can go home, but I'll probably just spend my time off dwelling on it there, too. I don't seem to be able to stop myself.

I drive across town with my head in the clouds. I should find a way to snap myself out of this. I just don't know how to.

I've been dwelling on that ever since John's death, too. I should ask Carter or the Brewers to help me, but I can't even find the words to do that.

It would be so easy to walk up to Carter and say, "Help me." That's less than I said to Jessie on that call today.

He would jump at the chance. I know he would. He would be more than happy to give me anything I needed—and he would be so cool about it. He's the best guy in the world.

I can't do that, though—or at least I haven't been able to do it yet. I get frozen the same way I get frozen by everything else.

Chapter 4: Ellis

I drive down the highway not thinking about too much of any-thing. I make it ten miles down the road toward my house when I happen to notice an overturned big rig on the side of the road.

I probably wouldn't have noticed it at all because it doesn't look like anything is happening over there.

None of the other cars stop and I don't see any Police or other emergency service vehicles or personnel around.

At first glance, it looks like the wreck must have happened a week ago or maybe more. Now everyone is gone leaving only the abandoned remains of the truck on the side of the road.

The truck isn't getting in anyone's way. Four lanes of traffic flow past it. No one even looks at the truck.

The wreck couldn't have happened a week ago. I would have heard about the fire crew attending a call like that. I haven't heard anything about an overturned big rig.

I pull my pickup over just to check, grab my emergency medical kit, and walk up to the rig. I have to climb all the way up the side of the cab so I can look through the passenger window.

I make it halfway up there when I hear voices behind me. They're too high-pitched to be adult voices and they're coming from the wrong direction.

Four lanes of traffic whizz past me just a few feet beyond the rig. Hundreds of miles of countryside spread out behind me. There shouldn't be anyone out here.

I glance over my shoulder. A steep embankment drops down behind the highway shoulder. Dense bushes crowd the bottom of the embankment in a deep ravine.

The voices definitely come from there, but I don't see anything or anyone.

Right then, the bushes rustle and I catch a glimpse of a passenger car lying buried at the bottom of the embankment. The voices are coming from the car. They're children's voices.

I grab my phone and use one hand to clamber the rest of the way up the rig. I take one look through the passenger window, spot the driver lying unconscious in his seat, and perch on top of the rig to call 911.

I hold the phone with one hand while I lower my upper body into the cab to check the driver's pulse.

"911 emergency dispatch," a smooth male voice greets me. "Please state the nature of the emergency."

"This is Ellis Barrett. I'm a firefighter with the Howe County Fire Department," I pant. "There's a big rig and a passenger car crashed on the side of the highway—at least four patients that I can see."

I press my fingers to the driver's neck. He still has a pulse.

"One moment, Sir," the operator tells me. "Is the scene secure for emergency personnel to gain access?"

"Yeah!" I gasp and drag myself out of the cab. I hustle down to the ground while I give the operator the location. "Everything is off on the shoulder. The truck driver is unconscious, but he's breathing and has a pulse. I'm just about to check on the passengers in the car."

"I'm dispatching fire, Police, and medical crews now," the operator tells me. "Please stay on the line."

I scramble down the embankment. I'm just glad no one from the fire crew is around to hear me make this call. They would all make a huge deal about me talking this much—like I would ever come across a crash like this and not make the call.

The embankment walls are too steep. I slide down there and my legs go through the foliage.

I land on top of the car. The talking stops immediately when the kids realize someone is here.

I push the branches out of the way with one hand and hold the phone to my ear with the other.

The car rests on its side at the bottom of the ravine. I look down through the open rear passenger window. Three little kids sit huddled on the opposite door and stare up at me with huge eyes.

I squat down and move the phone away from my ear while I listen for the operator's further instructions.

"Hey there!" I tell the kids. "I'm Ellis. I'm a firefighter with the Fire Department. Don't worry. The fire trucks and ambulances are coming to get you out. Are any of you hurt?"

"No, but they are." The oldest boy points to the driver's compartment. The kid can't be more than seven.

His parents lie unconscious in the driver's and front passenger seats.

"Can you help them?" a little girl asks.

"We didn't know what to do," the boy tells me. "We were just trying to decide."

"Don't worry," I tell them. "The ambulances will take your parents to the hospital. Come on. I'll get you out."

I hold out my hand, but right then, the operator comes back on. "Fire, Police, and medical crews are on the way, Sir. Please stay on the line until they arrive."

"I can't," I tell him. "There are three little kids in the car. I have to hang up to help them. I have my phone with me. You can call me back if you need to."

I get off the phone with him as quickly as I can. I can already hear sirens in the distance.

I squat down and extend both hands to the kids. "Come on up. We need to get out of the way so the Fire Department can help your parents. Give me your hands and I'll take you back up to the road."

The little girl stands up first. Her older brother pushes her up into my hands.

I lift her out, stand her on the side of the car, and brush the dust off her little dress while I study her face. "Did you get hurt anywhere? Is anything hurting?"

She shakes her head. "I want my mommy."

"I know, sweetie. We're gonna take care of her the best we can. Stay here while I get your brother and sister out."

The boy lifts out his other sister next and then I pull him up. I give all three the most superficial examination just to make sure they aren't hurt. They aren't.

"You climb on my back, son," I tell the boy.

He does it and straps his little arms around my neck tight enough to choke me, but I don't care.

I take the two little girls, one in each of my arms. "Now hold on tight. I'm going to climb out with you."

The girls cry and cling to me when I start climbing. I need to get them to safety before all the emergency workers start pulling the parents out of the car. I don't want the kids around for that.

I'm dripping with sweat and breathing heavily by the time I get to the top. I get there just as the Police cordon off two lanes of traffic and Keith backs the rescue truck up the shoulder.

I take the three kids over to the Police and give one of the officers a rundown on what I found. Then I have to do the same thing with Duke and Keith.

I catch a bunch of people on the fire crew giving me strange looks because I'm talking so much. I just have to push through it.

I'm just about to go help the crew winch the car out of the bushes, but I touch base with the three kids first. "Your parents probably have to go to the hospital to fix whatever is wrong with them. The Police officers will call someone to come and get you."

"Call my grandma," the oldest boy tells me.

"Okay, you tell the officers that and they'll call her. You tell them her name and maybe her phone number if you know it...."

"I don't know it."

"That's okay. The Police will be able to find it. They'll take care of you until she comes to get you. Everything is going to be okay now. You're safe."

"Will we ever see you again, Ellis?" the older girl asks.

I find myself smiling at her and touching her hair. "I hope so, sweetie. I'm just glad you're all okay. Now I have to go help the fire crew. We'll get your parents out and take them to the hospital, okay?"

"Bye, Ellis," the boy says.

I say goodbye to them all and head back to the crew. Keith and Billy are already setting up the outriggers to stabilize the rescue truck so they can winch the car onto level ground.

Theo Gough, Vince Jaeger, and Jacob Franks balance on top of the rig trying to extricate the driver through the open passenger window.

I head for the rescue truck to help with the car. I'm still wearing my uniform, so I fit right in. I plan to ask Duke where he wants to assign me, but the screech of car tires distracts me.

I don't even have time to turn around before a car breaks the Police cordon, plows into the scene, and runs right into me.

Chapter 5: Jessie

I walk into the hospital waiting room and stop when I see Ellen Foreman talking to Duke across the room. Keith stands over there with them and so do two doctors.

I hesitate to go over there, but concern about Ellis overcomes my reluctance.

Ellen smiles at me when I show up. "How is he?" I ask.

"He just woke up," Ellen tells me. "He's been in a coma for almost twenty-four hours. He has scrapes, bruises, and swelling all over his body from the collision, but no broken bones."

I wilt in relief. "Thank God he's all right!"

"I have to warn you. He isn't as all right as he seems. He lost his memory."

My head shoots up. "What? All of it?"

"No, not all of it. The psychiatry department still has to run some tests to find out exactly what he remembers and what he doesn't remember. I have to tell you right now, though. He's back to the way he was before John's death." She makes a face. "The nurses want to release Ellis as soon as possible. He won't stop making jokes and flirting with all the nurses, even the older ones."

I gape at her in disbelief. "You mean....he's back....just like that?"

"Not entirely. He doesn't remember any of what caused him to go silent in the first place. That's why he's acting like this. He doesn't remember anything from about the last year. You can go visit him. Then you'll be able to see for yourself. Just try not to be too shocked by the way he's acting."

I don't know what to say. I'm not sure I want to see Ellis completely switch back to his old self overnight.

The rest of the crew files down the hall and goes into one of the ward rooms. I go with them, but I let myself get lost in the crowd.

Duke, Keith, and Danny go first. The rest of the crew follows.

We fill Ellis's room and I immediately realize what Ellen was talking about.

Ellis looks up at us and bursts into a grin. "Look at this. It's the Four Horsemen of the Apocalypse! Did you bring plague, famine, disease....or just a whole bunch of emergencies?"

No one laughs. No one smiles. We line up in front of his bed.

His eyes dart around the room, but he only grins even more broadly at our reaction. "When can I get out of here? The nurses keep saying there's nothing wrong with me."

"There doesn't seem to be anything wrong with your sense of humor," Duke replies. "The nurses are complaining that you keep flirting with them."

Ellis laughs. "You can't blame me for having some fun with them, can you? There's nothing else to do in this place."

Duke stiffens and pulls himself up to his full height. "Do you know who I am, son?"

Ellis's head shoots up. He frowns at Duke and then laughs again. "Of course I know who you are. You're Duke Broebeck."

"What else am I? What am I that I would come and visit you in the hospital like this?"

Ellis blinks at him. "Um.....you're the Fire Chief....and you're my boss......" Ellis furrows his brow. "Is this a trick question?"

"Do you know who this is?" Duke waves at Carter.

"It's Carter Holt." Ellis starts to smile at Carter. Ellis definitely recognizes him. "What is this all about?"

"What about this?" Duke pulls Josh forward. "Do you know who this is?"

"It's Josh Abbott." Ellis grins at Josh. "Hey, buddy."

"Hey, man," Josh murmurs. "It's good to see that you're feeling better."

Ellis turns back to Duke. "Did I pass the test? Can I go home now?"

"Do you know why I'm here acting as Fire Chief instead of John Brewer?" Duke asks.

Ellis frowns at him. "I don't understand. What is this all about?"

"John is dead," Keith rumbles. "You don't remember, do you?"

Ellis's jaw drops in horror. He gapes at the Brewer brothers and then at all the rest of us. "Dead?!" he gasps. "He can't be!"

"You don't remember what you did for me?" Carter asks.

"Do you remember John hiring me?" Josh asks.

"Do you remember me starting work at the firehouse?" Duke asks.

Ellis's eyes dart from one person to the next. Then he gulps.

"You lost your memory," Duke tells him. "You've been under a cloud since John's death. You don't remember how it affected you."

Ellis's hand flies to his head. "My God! I can't believe he's dead!"

"Do you feel okay other than that?" Duke asks. "Ellen says the psychiatrists still need to run some tests on you."

"Forget all that!" Ellis insists. "I just want to get back out there and go back to saving the world." He flashes Duke a huge grin. "I'm good at that."

"You won't be saving anything until the doctors let you go," Duke replies. "They might find some underlying problem if this head injury caused such a massive change in your personality."

Ellis frowns at him again. "What do you mean? I feel fine."

Ellen interrupts just then by coming back into the room. "Ellis's parents are here to see him."

"We'll get out of your way." Duke turns back to Ellis. "I'll come and see you later and find out what's happening with your psych evaluations."

Ellis snorts. "That could turn out to be opening up a whole can of worms you don't want to mess with."

He laughs at his own joke, but he's the only one who does. The rest of the crew stares at him in shock.

He's acting exactly the way he acted before John's death, but his constant banter, smiling, and cheery attitude leaves me cold.

Duke is right. Something is wrong with Ellis. I almost liked him better when he was silent and distant. At least I knew that was genuine.

We file out of the room. Ellis catches me looking at him and smiles at me, but I can't smile back.

We meet Ellis's parents in the waiting room. A bunch of the crew step forward to hug them.

Patricia and Arlen Barrett are fixtures in the firehouse family. They always come to visit Ellis. His parents have even come to a few barbecues.

Patricia is a round, cherubic lady of fifty with apple cheeks and a rosy disposition. Her husband is portly, short, and extremely affable.

They know about my friendship with Ellis and they are always super nice to me. His mother kisses me on the cheek. "I was so worried when I heard he got hit by a car! I can't wait to see him!"

"Just don't be too shocked by the way he's acting," I tell her. "He's back to joking around and laughing at everything."

Her mouth drops open and she gasps out loud. "Is he, really? That's wonderful! Oh, thank Heaven!" She clasps her hands and tears come to her eyes. "He's been so sad since Chief Brewer died. Oh, it's a miracle! I can't wait to see him!"

She rushes off to Ellis's room. Arlen gives everyone on the crew his best and hurries after her.

A hush falls over the crew after they leave. We all stare toward the closed door leading to Ellis's hospital room.

"I don't believe it," Keith mutters. "I never would have believed he'd snap out of it so fast."

"He didn't," Duke remarks. "He's only acting like this because he doesn't remember what made him depressed in the first place. He'll get depressed again as soon as he does remember."

"He might never remember," Danny suggests.

"I find that difficult to believe," Duke replies. "People don't just forget something as important as that. If he suffered a traumatic brain injury serious enough to make him forget it for the rest of his life, it will affect him in other ways. You mark my words."

He walks out of the waiting room. There's nothing to do here but stand and stare. After another few minutes, the rest of the crew starts to leave, too.

I should do the same thing, but I don't seem to be able to tear myself away. I don't know what to do about Ellis, but I'm starting to agree with Duke.

This car accident didn't fix whatever is wrong with Ellis. Whatever caused him to go silent in the first place, it's still in there haunting him. It will come back to the surface one way or the other.

Chapter 6: Ellis

I stroll into the firehouse and grin when I see the crew standing around talking. "Where's the fire? Ha ha!" I try to laugh, but no one reacts.

"You're on the rescue truck with us today," Keith tells me. "Try not to fall over yourself acting like an idiot."

"When have I ever acted like an idiot?" I counter. "I might have acted like an insufferable clod, but never an idiot."

No one laughs at that, either. I'm starting to get worried because no one even smiles. They all stare at me in what I can only describe as suspicious horror.

I don't understand why everyone is acting so weird around me all of a sudden. My parents made a few passing remarks at the hospital that confirmed what Duke said about how I supposedly reacted to John Brewer's death.

I still don't understand why everyone is so down around me. Some of the crew will barely look at me.

I try to get back to normal. "So who else is rostered on the truck with us?"

"Billy, Danny, and Caleb are in the front with us," Keith tells me. "Jessie and Sophie are in the back."

"Hey!" I elbow Jessie, who stands next to me. "Just like old times, huh? Don't worry. I'll protect you from these heathens."

She makes eye contact with me for a split second before she looks away. She tries to smile and fails. Her expression comes off more as a grimace.

I stand there blinking down at the side of her head. She can't be acting weird around me, too—not after we've been so close all these years.

I thought she would be the easiest to get back into our old routine, but she actually acts even more standoffish than the rest of the crew.

Keith breaks in on my thoughts. "You better get busy with your truck checks. The world won't save itself."

The crew breaks up with everyone going off to different vehicles. I'm more than happy to take the focus off myself and get back to work, but I catch plenty of my co-workers giving me strange looks as they walk away.

I put my stuff away in my locker and go back to the rescue truck to find Caleb and Billy already in there. Jessie and Sophie sit in the back talking and going over their gear.

I get ready to climb up there, too, but Keith grabs me and assigns me to do the inspection of the truck's exterior. I'm just finishing that when I see Jessie go off to the supply room for something.

I hustle after her and slide in there behind her.

I give her my best grin. "Hey!"

She glances at me and then goes back to pulling syringes off the shelf. "Hey," she replies over her shoulder. "I guess you passed all your psych evaluations or you wouldn't be back at work."

I try to make a joke about it to lighten the mood. "Don't tell me you wanted me to fail my evaluations. I'm not that psycho, am I?"

Her eyes dart in my direction one more time. "Your swelling looks like it's going down."

"What the hell is wrong with everyone around here?" I blurt out. "Why is everyone tiptoeing around me like I just came back from beyond the grave or something?"

She turns her back on me to get some bandages out of a different compartment. "Maybe you did."

"What is that supposed to mean? What's wrong? You won't even look at me. Did I do something wrong? Is that what's going on? Did I do something really bad in the last year that I don't remember and no one wants to tell me what I did?" I try to laugh that off, too. "Don't tell me I had something to do with John's death."

She freezes in mid-motion and then turns around extra slowly. She finally looks at me, but the look in her eyes makes my blood run cold.

I can't remember her ever looking at me like this. She's scaring me.

I gulp. "I did, didn't I? I had something to do with John's death. Just tell me the truth."

"No, you didn't. You had nothing to do with his death."

"What is it, then? Did I kill someone...or hurt someone?" My stomach drops into my shoes. "Did I do something to hurt you, sweetie? I swear I didn't mean to if I did."

"No, Ellis," she murmurs. "You didn't do anything to hurt me or anyone else."

"Will you please just tell me what I did? Now I'm really worried."

She takes a deep breath. "You had nothing to do with John's death. Andy Skinner got really jealous of Carter when Carter and Sophie started getting interested in each other. Andy and Sophie hadn't been a thing for years, but Andy developed a vendetta against Carter and tried to kill him by sabotaging his SCBA right before a dangerous call. Andy got charged with attempted murder."

I frown at her. "I don't remember any of that. What does this have to do with me?"

She takes another deep breath. I've never seen her so serious. "Andy got himself released on bail and showed up at the barbecue with a gun. He tried to shoot Carter. You tackled Andy out of the way just as the gun went off. You saved Carter's life."

I brighten up. "Oh. Well, that's a good thing, right? I wouldn't want some psycho to kill Carter."

"Yes, it was a very good thing that you saved Carter's life. The problem was that the bullet that would have hit Carter hit John instead. That's how he died. You blamed yourself for his death. You've spent the last few months extremely depressed and isolated. You wouldn't talk to anyone or even look at us. You stopped coming to the barbecues except when you were rostered on duty and you had to come. You....." Tears well up in her dark eyes. "I was so worried about you....and n ow...."

"Hey! I'm here. I'm all right." I walk into the supply room and hug her. "I'm all right now. You can see I'm not depressed."

She pushes me away and passes her hand across her eyes. "You aren't all right. I don't know what happened, but this isn't you. That's why everyone is so uncomfortable around you. It's taken us all so long to get used to you being silent and distant all the time.....and now you just suddenly changed back overnight....."

"If everyone was worried about me and uncomfortable around me before, then they should all be happy that I'm back, right?"

"You aren't back, Ellis!" she snaps and immediately corrects herself. "Don't you get it? Whatever made you withdraw in the first place—it's still there. You didn't just magically get over whatever caused you to change your personality. You don't even remember John's death, do you?"

"Well, no, but from the way you talk about it, it sounds like something I don't want to remember."

"That's what I'm talking about. Something happened to you when John died and it didn't just unhappen when you lost your memory. You could get your memory back and then you would be right back to being that way."

I frown at her trying to understand what she's saying. I guess I can't argue with her logic.

She turns back to gathering things off the shelf. "I can't decide if I liked you better that way or like this. At least when you were like that, I could understand what you were doing and why. I wanted to help you, but now, it's like you aren't even real. I don't know who this person is, but you aren't the person I knew."

"How can I not be? If I lost my memory of the last year, then I'm back to being the person I was a year ago. We were still friends then, weren't we?"

"A lot happened this last year," she mutters without turning around. "The last year changed all of us. I'm not sure I want to go back to a year ago."

"You wouldn't want to go back to when John was still alive?" I ask.

"John isn't alive," she snaps over her shoulder. "John isn't coming back. Whatever caused you to lose your memory didn't just magically bring him back. You're forgetting something that actually happened—something important to all of us. It was just as important to you. You aren't normal like this. I don't know what normal is, but you won't be normal until you remember what happened and how it affected you."

Chapter 7: Ellis

I come downstairs from Duke's office where I've just been giving him chapter and verse on the results of my psych evaluations at the hospital.

The doctors can't find anything wrong with me apart from my memory loss. I didn't forget my job training, so I'm cleared to return to work unless something changes.

Duke also gave me the details of the call where I got hit by a car. I don't remember that, either, but he says I saved five people, including three young children.

He says he's going to put me in for a decoration for that, but he doesn't act happy about it. No one around here acts happy about anything when it comes to me.

I don't know how to act around any of them, either, but that hardly matters. I'm back at work.

Hopefully everyone will get used to this in time and we can all go on as normal.

There's that word again. Normal. Jessie says I'm not normal even though I feel fine.

The firehouse alarm goes off when I'm halfway down the stairs. I'm already off shift, so the second shift goes out in the vehicles.

Everyone else from the morning shift is already gone—or so I think. I walk into the locker room to get my stuff and automatically grin when I see Jessie there.

I go over to her. "I've been meaning to ask you—do you want to go out with me sometime? We could go to the fun park and play minigolf or ride the go-karts or whatever. We always have fun with that, don't we?"

She looks up and her eyes widen. "You're asking me out—like for real—not just to go out as friends? Would this be an actual....like.... date?"

I burst into a smile and feel my cheeks burning. "Can you blame me? You know I like you and you like me. What are we waiting for?"

She turns away shaking her head. "I don't think that's a good idea, Ellis."

"Why?" I grab her arm and turn her around. "Come on. I've been meaning to ask you out for ages."

She stares at me again. "You have? You never said anything before."

"Well, I should have. I kick myself for not asking you sooner. Getting hurt made me realize I can't waste any more time." I take a chance and raise my hand to gently caress a stray lock of her hair out of her face.

She's beyond adorable and she's one of my closest friends. I've always been sweet on her. I'm an idiot for leaving it so long without asking her out.

She stares at me in shock and I get a stomach load of adrenaline looking into her eyes. I want to kiss her right this minute.

We've always been really close friends, but I want to take it further.

Her lips tremble when I touch her face. What does she see when she looks at me? Is it possible she likes me as much as I like her? Has she been dreaming about me all this time the way I've been dreaming about her?

She finally looks away. "I don't think this is a good idea, Ellis."

"Why not? If you're right that I was like this before, then this must be what's normal to me. Getting hit by the car must have put me back into my normal state. Are you worried I'll go back to being quiet? I'm not that way now. Why can't we just go out and enjoy the way things are now?"

"This can't be what's normal for you, Ellis," she tells me. "You didn't want to go out with me when you were quiet. Remembering everything that happened in the last year would make you remember that you didn't want to go out with me."

"Would you have gone out with me before I changed and got quiet?" I ask.

"Yes, I would have. I always liked you."

"Did you stop liking me when I was quiet and went off by myself? Would you have gone out with me then if I asked you?"

"No, I didn't stop liking you. I always liked you even then. I just wanted to help you."

"Then, if you liked me both ways and wanted to go out with me both ways, then it shouldn't matter how I act and you should go out with me regardless." I grin at her. "Ha. Gotcha!"

She starts grinning back at me and tries unsuccessfully to bite it back. "Did you really want to go out with me before?"

"Of course!" I think fast to come up with a joke to make her laugh, but I change my mind instead.

I ease in and raise my hand. I at first plan to trace my fingers through her hair, but I end up very gently clasping my hand around her face instead.

I lift her mouth to mine and kiss her. She tastes immaculate—exactly the way I knew she would.

"You're gorgeous and sweet....and you've always been the one person I've been closest to," I murmur. "I don't want to wait anymore. I want to go out with you and take it further....if you let me."

She kisses me back—just once, very lightly.

I don't want to push it too far, so I step away and put my hand down.

She blinks up at me with so many conflicting emotions raging in her eyes. I can't decide if I should be happy or sad that she's so confused about me.

Whatever kind of disaster made her so uncomfortable around me? Whatever it was, I can't ever let it happen again.

I just want to put her back to the way she was before—warm, fun-loving, vivacious.

I can't rewrite the last year. I don't even know what happened to these people in the last year, but it must have been absolutely catastrophic to change the firehouse so much.

I back off just a little more. "I'll call you, okay?" I tell her.

She gives me a full smile—just like she did before. "Okay."

I get out of there as quickly as I can and race home with my heart all a-flutter. I can't believe this is actually happening. I'm going out with Jessie.

I go through my house and put everything in order, but I can't find much wrong with the place. Whatever I've been doing with myself over the past year, I certainly didn't fall off on taking care of my house.

I didn't fall off on taking care of myself, either. I'm bigger, more cut, and I can lift more weight than I could a year ago.

I surprise myself when I go back to the firehouse and do a workout. I follow the notes in my workout journal. I've been very diligent and strict with both my workout schedule and my nutrition plan.

The guys don't act as stiff around me in the gym as they do on shift—maybe because I don't try so hard to talk, joke, and lighten the mood. We all just work out like we're supposed to.

Josh and Carter are in there, too. I find myself studying both of them. I remember them, but I can't remember the events of how or when they got hired.

I've seen the way they act around Chris and Sophie. Both of these men are married now, but I don't remember any of that, either. Maybe Jessie has a point about all of this.

A lot must have happened over the last year. If it changed them, it must have changed me, too. It may even have changed me more than she says it did.

I can't think about that when I know I'm going to go out with her. I have to fight myself not to text her until I get off my shift the following night.

I find my hands shaking when I finally do text her. *You have tomorrow night off, don't you? Do you want to go out then? I could pick you up at seven.*

She texts back right away. *I'd like that. See you then.*

My heart flips when I read her text. She actually wants to go out with me. Why did I wait so long to ask her?

I have to get through another night by myself and then another shift before our date. I indulge in fantasizing about her the night before. I've never done that before. I never let myself even think about her that w ay.

Now the genie is out of the bottle and it won't go back in.

I have to work with her during the shift on the big day, but we both pretend like it isn't happening. I would have thought we were both acting weird by avoiding each other, but it only seems normal considering what's about to happen.

I'm a nervous wreck by the time I go home. I take a hot shower and change my clothes. I don't wear a full-on suit. I wouldn't wear a suit to the fun park.

I go with casual khakis and a black button-up shirt under a casual bomber jacket. This is nothing I wouldn't have worn with her every other time we've gone out as friends.

It's also nothing I wouldn't wear on a real date with any other woman I don't see every day at the firehouse.

I decide to dress up my outfit by wearing nicely polished black leather boots instead of sneakers—which is what I would have worn if I went out with her any other time as friends.

I pick her up at the stroke of seven and nearly have a heart attack when I see what she's wearing.

She comes out of her apartment wearing a tight, thigh-length black dress that absolutely knocks my socks off. The thin spaghetti straps leave her chest exposed down to just above her cleavage.

She wears tiny black ballet flats on her feet and a small, tight, black beaded jacket that covers her arms to just below the elbows.

A delicate gold chain graces her neck and collarbones. My mouth starts to water when I see her dark hair hanging loose and brushing her neck and the top of her bare chest. God, I want to get my hands on her.

She blushes when she sees me gawking at her with my jaw on the floor. She never would have worn something like this when we went out as friends.

We aren't going out as friends. That's more than obvious.

"Put your eyes back in their sockets," she teases.

"Wow!" I gasp. "You look delicious."

She turns bright red and looks away. "Let's not start talking like that so early in the set. Let's go."

Chapter 8: Ellis

I lead Jessie out to my truck. I'm too stunned by how magnificently hot she is to think of anything witty to say.

I open the door for her to get in. I find myself staring at her again when she settles herself in the passenger seat and buckles her seatbelt.

I hardly recognize her like this. This is not the warm, friendly paramedic I've been working with at the firehouse all these years.

This is some kind of vixen I met under mysterious circumstances. This is some kind of apparition sweeping into my life on a wave of passion—an apparition who will disappear into the shadows just as fast.

Thinking of her like that lights my fire as never before. I feel myself starting to get hard just from looking at her.

Are we going to have torrid romance that ends in a fiery explosion of drama and broken dreams?

I have to get my head screwed on straight when I walk around the truck to get behind the wheel. I can't look at her while I drive.

I don't want this to end in a fiery explosion of drama and broken dreams. I want....her. I want this to be real.

I don't want to think of her as a mysterious stranger who sweeps into and out of my life just as fast. I want Jessie....but this is her. This goddess is my friend—the woman I thought was my friend.

Out of nowhere, her small, delicate hand comes to rest on my shoulder while we drive. "I'm really glad you're okay," she murmurs. "I was really worried when Duke told me you were in the hospital."

I gulp when I hear the quaver in her voice. She has never talked to me with as much emotion as I've been hearing from her these last few days.

I never realized she cared about me so deeply. I always knew we were friends and we liked each other. It never went deeper than that.

I have to fight my own voice under control to talk to her. "I'm really sorry if the way I've been acting these last few months hurt your feelings. I mean....it obviously did hurt your feelings and I'm sorry. I never would have done anything to hurt you—not knowingly."

"I just wish I could believe it was real," she murmurs. "I wish like anything I could believe that you were back to your real self. I'm sorry if I acted weird around you when you first got out of the hospital. I just....I don't know what's real and what isn't when it comes to you."

I pull into the fun park, switch off the motor, and finally let myself face her. I can't hide from her, especially not if we're going to have something real the way I want us to.

I take her hand off my shoulder and cradle her hand between both of mine. I want to radiate into her how I feel about her.

"I only want to be real with you from now on," I tell her. "I don't want anything between us."

She looks up at me and her features spasm before she looks away. "I wish I could believe it was really you saying that."

"It is me. It's my heart saying it."

She still won't look at me, so I take a chance, cup her chin, and turn her face around so she has no choice but to look straight into my eyes.

"I don't know what I did or said or didn't say in the last year, but how I feel about you is real," I breathe. "It always has been and it always will be. Whatever I did during the last year, I promise you I still cared about you. I still wanted this with you even if I never told you so. I might have pushed you away for some other reason, but how I feel about you didn't change. This is real. What's between us right now is r eal."

Tears spring back to her eyes. My stomach hurts when I realize that she's tearing up because she cares about me that much.

"I just want it to be real!" she chokes. "I was so worried that I lost you—that we all lost you. You were so distant.....and I tried so hard to bring you back.....and you never responded to me.....you wouldn't even look at me......"

Her tears streak down her cheeks. My heart breaks watching her.

"Hey! I'm right here with you!"

I want to hug her, but when I try, the truck seats separate us too much. I wind up lifting her out of her seat and pulling her into my lap.

I cradle her while she cries on my shoulder. I did hurt her. I know that now. I hate myself for that, but I still don't know why I did it.

She wants me. She might even love me. In fact, I know she does. She wouldn't hurt so badly from losing me if she didn't love me.

I kiss her hair and pet her arms to comfort her. I have to make this up to her. I have to be there for her in ways I wasn't before. I can't let her think I don't want her because I do. I would give anything to have something real with her.

I pull her head into my neck even after she stops crying. I've never touched her or held her like this before, but it feels right. Everything we're doing feels right and natural even though we're going so far beyond what we would ever dare to do before.

She finally sniffs and lies still. I wait until she completely calms down.

"Could you tell me a little more about why I did what I did?" I ask. "Can you give me more of a clue about what pushed me over the edge like that?"

She sits up on my lap. Her face looks puffy, but she's still gorgeous. "It was just what I already told you. You broke down John's funeral. We were all walking up to the church and you freaked out and said you couldn't go in there to face the Brewers because you were the one who caused John's death. I tried to talk to you and then Carter stepped in and told you that you were a hero for saving his life and he wouldn't be here if not for you. He talked you into going through the funeral—and that's the last time you really talked to anyone—about anything. The n.....the day before the car accident, you and I got isolated on a call and you talked to me. You told me something that saved my life and my patients' lives.....and then you talked a lot on that call where you got the kids out of their car—but you only did it because you had to. You had to give reports to Duke and the Police and talk to the patients and everything. You keep away from everyone apart from that. You don't talk unless you absolutely have to—and you never go out with us, not even to the barbecues."

I stare across the parking lot without seeing anything. "It doesn't sound like me at all. It sounds like you're talking about a completely different person."

"That's what I'm telling you. You have been a different person. It's been almost as hard to adjust to how different you are as it has been to get used to John not being here."

"I'm really sorry I hurt you like that, sweetie. I wish I could take it all back."

I look over at her to find her staring at me at short range.

She looks at me so differently now than she ever did before. She studies me with a penetrating, searching look like she's trying to figure me out.

She never had to figure me out before. She always knew me.

"What's wrong?" I ask. "You know I would never do anything like that now."

She doesn't seem to hear me. She's studying me too intently.

I become aware that she's sitting on my lap in a drop-dead-gorgeous black minidress. It's dark—almost romantic. She's right here in front of me.

I take a chance and kiss her again. This kiss turns into a steadily rising torrent of passion and smoking desire. I want to tear her clothes off and drill her right here on the seat of my truck.

I won't do that, though, but every inch of her that I lay my hands on lights me on fire like nothing else.

I content myself with cradling her cheeks, slipping my fingers into her hair, and pulling her closer to me by her back, hips, and the safe outer edge of her thighs.

My hand falls on the bare skin of her legs and she trembles in my grasp. Her body quivers with energy, but I don't let it go any further than that. I'm kissing her. That's enough.

She falls back in my arms and wraps her arms around my neck to pull me into her lips. My mind turns a somersault thinking about all the ways I could touch her and excite her and make her scream right now.

I force myself to pull back and gaze into her deep, mysterious eyes. "I meant what I said," I murmur under my breath. "How I felt about you never changed. It could never change no matter how I was acting."

She smiles, but her lips wrench again when her eyes well up. "How I felt about you never changed, either. It just made me care about you more."

I stroke her cheeks once. "Let's go have some fun. We don't need to dwell on that anymore."

I ease her over to her seat and get out of the truck. I have to fight myself under control to cool my blood down so I can behave on this date.

She straightens her clothes and checks her appearance in the visor mirror before I open her door for her. She smiles much more genuinely when she gets out.

Chapter 9: Ellis

Jessie and I set off toward the fun park, and like something out of a dream, she slips her hand into mine.

That feeling of her skin touching me sends a tendril of fire straight to my guts. I want so much with her. I want it all.

I want so much more than her body. I want her in my life, in my bed, in my kitchen, in my heart. I want her to be my everything for the rest of forever.

I can't tell her that tonight, though.

"What do you want to do first?" I ask. "Do you want to golf, play video games, eat, ride the go-karts—what?"

"Are you hungry—or do you want to do stuff first and eat afterward?"

I smirk at her. "I asked you first. Don't think you're going to get out of it by flipping the question back on me."

She bursts into another big blushing smile. "Fine. Be all commanding and masculine about it."

I laugh. "What did you think I was going to be—timid and subservient?"

She laughs with me. "A girl can dream."

"You better take that back right now. Don't you dare insult my manhood."

Her eyes pop and all the color drains from her cheeks. "Your man-hood? Seriously?"

"I meant my masculinity. You said it, not me. I wasn't talking about...you know....."

She bursts out laughing and her dark eyelashes dip when she blushes again. She looks intoxicating when she blushes like that.

"You still didn't answer my question," I tell her. "Do you want to do stuff first and eat afterward or the other way around?"

She looks away and bites her lip. "Well, I haven't eaten yet. I was waiting to see what you wanted to do."

"Why didn't you say so?"

I lead her to the food court where we get two loaded hot dogs, fries, and an ice cream sundae each.

This doesn't fit with my nutrition plan, but it's a special occasion. If my workout journal is right, this is the first time in over two years that I've gone off my plan. I can afford it based on what I've seen in the mirror.

Jessie giggles when she takes a bite of her hotdog and gets mustard on her nose. I pretend not to see her stuffing her mouth full of a long, cylindrical tube of sizzling hot meat.

Her lips intoxicate me. I get distracted by her tongue licking the relish off her lips and her mouth closing around her fries. I want to crawl into that mouth and die there.

Fortunately, we finish our meal before I completely lose control of myself.

We head out to the fun park afterward and I don't have any problem distracting myself while we ride the go-karts and play games in the arcade.

It gets a little harder when we play a round of minigolf and I see her bending over all the time. Did her ass just become suddenly rounder and more appealing or does her dress just make it seem that way?

I can't remember ever noticing her body this much. I can't remember ever thinking about her body at all.

It was her personality I liked so much. Maybe that's why I never asked her out. I was too taken with her as a friend. I never really thought of her as a hot, sexy, attractive woman I might dream about and want to make out with.

I don't have a hard time coming up with a steady stream of jokes to keep her entertained and laughing through the whole date. This doesn't even really feel like a date. If we hadn't just kissed in my truck, I could convince myself that we're still just friends.

Our interaction in public doesn't change that much from what I remember. She's just as fun-loving and easy-going as always.

We finally exhaust every available form of immature frivolity in the fun park and head back to the parking lot.

I might have convinced myself that we're just friends having fun, but she dispels that in an instant when she takes my hand again.

The illusion shatters the rest of the way as we get to the truck. She isn't my friend—not anymore. She's that witchy, intoxicating vixen who makes my blood boil.

I stop her next to the passenger door and turn her around to kiss her. We start kissing madly again without any of the soft, gentle, romantic prelude.

She comes at me just as passionately, wraps her arms around my neck, and doesn't hold back when I lift her off the ground to inhale her.

Her body blows my mind so much that I take a step forward and pin her against the truck. I claw at her body and wind up grabbing her thighs.

Every instinct in my being tells me to push up her dress, get between her legs, and grind my package into her until I plunge inside her.

Fortunately, my brain still functions well enough to stop me from doing that.

She gives a pathetic little whimper of desire when I drag my fingertips up her thighs, but I never make it past the lower hem of her dress. I stop there and just satisfy myself with kissing her.

I don't know if I'll ever do it with her. I'm not sure I want to. She's too perfect.

I lower her to the ground, but I don't stop kissing her and she doesn't let go of me.

She opens her mouth and her tongue dissolves my mind in sweetness. The heat of her kisses floods my being. My God, she is so perfect!

All things must come to an end, though, and she doesn't show any sign of slowing down.

I ease off, stroke her hair out of her eyes, and then kiss her on the forehead before I open the passenger door.

She settles on the seat and I drive her home. I walk her to her apartment door and kiss her some more before I straighten up to say good night.

Her fingers trail through my hand. I don't want to let her go, but I have to. I know that now. I have to let her go home and I have to go home to my place. This date can only end one way.

She reads my mind. "Do you want to come inside?" she asks.

"I would love to come inside, but I don't want this date to end like that. I mean, I do want this date to end like that, but I don't want us to go in that direction—not yet. I don't want this date to be about that.

I just want to be with you and for you to understand how I feel about you."

Her haunted dark eyes lift to meet mine. She hypnotizes me with her mysterious magical power. "Which direction do you want us to go?"

I kiss her again just to make my point. "What I just said. I want you to understand how I feel about you."

She gets lost in kissing me back for a minute before she can answer. "You definitely accomplished that tonight."

"You're beautiful and sweet.....and I love you as much as I ever did. I want you to know that. I can say that, can't I? We say it all the time....."

"Not like that, though. We never said it like that. Is that what you're saying—that you love me that way—or do you mean it as a friend?"

I straighten up to look down at her. I never realized how much taller I am than she is. She's right. It makes me feel much more dominant and masculine when I look down at her from above.

"You might not have been saying it that way all this time, but I was," I tell her. "Or maybe things changed for me when I got hit by that car. I only know how I feel about you now."

"Which is what?" she asks. "What is different—apart from the fact that we're kissing and holding hands now?"

I try to come up with the words to say how I feel about her, but instead, I just kiss her. I cradle the back of her head and press my hand against her back to bring her body right up against me.

I unload all my ravenous devouring passion into that kiss, but I don't take it any further. If she can't feel how much I want her through that kiss, telling her in words won't accomplish anything.

My breath catches as the energy sweeps through my body. I pant into her mouth and she matches me exactly. She gasps and then moans when I rock her against me and slide my hands all over her.

I finally break away and rest my forehead against hers while I catch my breath. Her body drives me wild. I want to explode in her right now, but I won't let myself do that.

"Now do you see?" I choke in a half-whisper. "Do you know how much I want you? I want you so bad."

"Ellis!" she whimpers. "Please come inside!"

"I can't, sweetheart. I want to. God knows I want to, but I can't. Not tonight. We'll get there, but I need to know you're safe and protected." I kiss her one last time. "Go inside before you give me a heart attack."

"Ellis....." She gets lost in kissing me again. "I......I love you."

My heart cracks at those words. I've always known she loved me. I just never let myself believe she loved me that way.

I always told myself she loved me as a friend—and she does. She still loves me as a friend, but now we love each other a different way. I just don't know how it's all going to play out. I guess I'm about to find out.

I force myself to straighten up before I lose my mind completely. My resolve is really starting to crack. I have to leave now.

I run my fingers through her hair one more time. "Go inside, baby. I had a wonderful time tonight and it's only the first of many. We'll go out again soon. We don't have to do everything tonight."

Her features jerk, but she doesn't try to tempt me again to go inside with her. I would probably cave if she did.

I kiss her one more time and she turns away to unlock the door. I stand back and watch until she turns around.

I kiss her again, but I keep it light and she backs away. She goes inside and shuts the door so I can't see her anymore.

Now it's my turn to walk away. I get a sudden thrill of exhilaration on my way back to my truck. I jump in the air and pump my fist in a silent cheer of victory.

Mmm-mmmm. Jessie Nash.

She is so sweet—and now she's mine—or she's going to be. I'll make sure of it.

Chapter 10: Jessie

I come out of my apartment and find Ellis standing at the door wearing jeans, sneakers, and a dark blue T-shirt tucked in under his leather jacket.

His T-shirt isn't a Fire Department T-shirt, but it still shows off his physique just as well.

He's been working out a lot more these last few years and he really threw himself into it after John died. The results speak for themselves.

My eyes dip to his clothes. "You said you wanted to take me to the barbecue as your date. You aren't dressed for a date—not the way you were before."

"This is a beach date." His eyes dip to my tight white capri pants, small white tennis shoes, and the white blouse under my beige blazer. I'm wearing my hair down again. "You look outstanding even like that. You always do."

I blush and look away. "I was trying to keep it understated."

"You did."

I let the subject drop, but he starts it right up again by taking my hand. He leads me outside to his truck and drives across town to the beach.

We get there at the same time as the two fire trucks and the two ambulances. Ellis has to wait before he can park.

By the time he does and takes his shopping bags out of the back, everyone is already down on the sand. We're the last two people to show up.

I hug Ellen and Leila and we talk about their families while Ellis puts his bags on the picnic table. I get distracted when baby Leon starts fussing and Leila has to shift him into a different position in her arms.

Naomi stands not far away. Leon's cries set Amelia off and the two mothers laugh together. "They speak each other's language," Naomi teases.

"Maybe we can get them to translate for us," Leila suggests and they laugh some more.

I get distracted by catching up with the three of them before I notice that Ellis isn't joining in. I turn around to see where he is and see him standing alone by the picnic table.

I go over to him. "You okay? Is something wrong?"

He stares across the beach. "What's the matter with her?"

I follow his gaze to where Oakleigh Brewer sits alone in the dunes. She keeps her back to the waves and the mass of kids running around playing. She bows her head below the sedge grass so no one can see what she's doing.

I slip my hand into his, squeeze some of my warmth into him, and lower my voice. "This is what I was trying to tell you in the supply room. Nothing has been the same since John's death. She's having a really hard time. She doesn't participate in the barbecues anymore—kind of like you stopped participating. She doesn't want to be here. It's taking her a lot longer to adjust to her dad not being around anymore."

He doesn't say anything for a long time. He just stares across the dunes at Oakleigh.

Does he see himself in her? Does he realize now that he can't just turn back the clock and make everything the way it was before John died?

I squeeze his hand again. "Come on. Come over here and talk to a few people. Everyone missed you. Maybe that will help."

He follows me and we head for the circle of crew members standing around talking. I go first, but before we get there, we run into Ellen and the two mothers again.

Ellis walks right up to Ellen. "Hey, sweetie! Long time, no see." He puts his arms around her and hugs her. "How's life at the hospital?"

She freezes in shock. She stands rigid and waits for him to let go of her. She doesn't hug him back.

When he straightens up to smile at her, she just stares at him with her eyes hanging out. Her expression goes through multiple rapid shifts. She doesn't speak or respond to his affection.

He smiles at her waiting for her to say something....and then glances around to find Leila and Naomi staring at him in something like horror. Both mothers clutch their babies.

Ellis's cheery smile slips slightly and then he glances at me in confusion. I squeeze his hand again. "Try to take it easy with the affection, okay? No one is used to the way you're acting after you've been quiet and distant for so long."

He notices Leon and Amelia as if for the first time. "When did that happen?"

I drag him away with an effort. "Come on. We can talk about it later."

We leave the three mothers alone. I try not to notice when they immediately put their heads together and start whispering about Ellis behind his back. We're going to get a lot of that here.

I take him over to the circle where Josh, Chris, Sophie, Carter, Brooke, Billy, Theo, Duke, and Danny stand around talking with Caleb and Allison.

"I don't see why the State Commission has to change the regulations at all," Chris is saying. "The dosage rates worked fine before."

"You didn't hear about the case where someone with an allergy Malazopan died from an overdose?" Allison asks. "The family petitioned the State Commission to change the rules."

"That makes no sense at all," Chris counters. "Did they die of an allergic reaction or did they die from an overdose?"

"The news release didn't say, but the clinical findings must have been enough to get the commission to change it."

"Maybe the patient wasn't allergic to Malazopan," Josh suggests. "Maybe they were allergic to something else and the old dosage triggered the reaction which caused the death. Maybe that's why they changed the dosage."

"Just don't include any of that in my next professional development assessment," Billy adds. "I can't keep my oxygen flow rates straight. I'll never understand how you can remember all those drugs. It's a good thing epi pens come pre-loaded or I would be in trouble."

A few people laugh.

"Who has a funny call they want to talk about?" Danny asks.

"We got a call last night when an old lady pushed her medical emergency alarm because her fridge light getting burned out," Sophie replies. "She used the light to get to and from her bedroom when she wanted to get up and get herself some munchies in the middle of the night without turning on the main overhead light."

"Then we got had to check the defibrillator at the funeral home," Brooke adds. "Something tells me the dead people won't be needing it."

"What about the old guy who complained of chest pain because he had his belt hitched up too high around his ribs?" Ellis asks.

No one laughs. An uncomfortable silence falls over the group. Danny walks away to go over to the barbecue. He relieves Keith.

The awkward tension in the group doesn't ease until Keith joins us. "You can all line up at the filling station to have your arteries hardened now," he announces.

A bunch of people take him up on the offer, and just then, Leila comes over and hands off Leon to Keith.

Keith kisses his son, puts the baby on his shoulder, and holds him there in his big, beefy arms while Leila goes off to the parking lot—probably to go to the bathroom.

"So where did you find it?" Ellis asks Keith. "Did someone leave it in a dumpster?"

Keith glares at him. "Do yourself a favor, kid. Keep your mouth shut the way you have the last couple of months."

Ellis turns white. "I was just trying to start a conversation."

"Well, don't start a conversation. You're only making an ass out of yourself."

Leon squawks just then and Keith turns the baby around, sits him facing outward, and holds him with one arm across Leon's chest.

I find myself beaming at the baby boy. "He's gorgeous, Keith. He sure is getting big. He can make eye contact so much better now."

"He smiles a lot more now, too. Watch this."

Keith flips the baby back around to face himself, takes hold of Leon with both big hands around the baby's torso, lifts Leon over his head, and swoops the baby back and forth in flying motions.

"I'm flying!" Keith sings in an overly high voice. "Look, Mom! I'm flying through the air with the greatest of ease! I'm a bird! I'm a plane! I'm Super-Leon!"

Keith flexes his arms up and down with the movements, tips Leon's head toward the ground, and flies the baby past his face to kiss Leon under the chin before hoisting the baby back to full height.

I laugh....and then Leon bursts out laughing. He only does it for a second, but he breaks into a delightful smile.

"Amelia likes that, too," Duke chimes in. "She really likes it when I lie on my back on the floor and balance her on the bottom of my feet to hold her above the ground."

Keith pumps Leon up and down in a bench press movement and sings, "Bring Sally up! Bring Sally down! Bring Leon up! Bring Leon down!" The baby laughs again and a few other people join in.

"Don't drop him on his head," Ellis tells him.

Keith pretends not to hear. He lowers Leon back toward his face where Keith plunges his scruffy face into Leon's soft, chubby neck. Keith roots around in there making guttural grunting and gnawing noises and makes Leon laugh again.

I find myself giggling. "He's adorable."

Keith puts the baby back in the crook of his elbow and leans the baby against his shoulder so they can both calm down and catch their breath.

"And that, ladies and gentlemen, is how it's done," Duke remarks. "Learn from the best."

Keith shoots him a blushing smile. "It's all trial and error, pal—mostly error—a lot of error."

The conversation turns and different people wander off to different parts of the barbecue. I get swept into a few different clusters and then back into the main circle.

The crew is just joking around again about the old lady who called the Fire Department for a blown-out refrigerator light.

We all laugh about it—and then I notice that Ellis isn't here anymore.

I look around and spot him near the parking lot. I could brush that off by thinking he went to the bathrooms, but something doesn't feel right.

I go over there and find him leaning against his truck fender drinking out of his beer bottle.

"What's wrong?" I ask. "What are you doing over here?"

He looks up at me and his eyes flash with dangerous fire. "You said I didn't have anything to do with John's death."

"You didn't! I told you what happened."

"Then why are the Brewers treating me like some kind of freak? Ellen wouldn't hug me and then Keith just told me to keep my mouth shut. Danny would barely even look at me."

"I told you why. Nothing has been the same since John died."

"That doesn't mean anything. They're all treating me like they think I had something to do with it."

I open my mouth to reassure him again that he didn't.

The words die on my lips when a million puzzle pieces click into place. Duke's words come back to me out of a bad dream.

He says Ellis was immature before. His sense of humor was inappropriate. He said the wrong things at the wrong times and made people uncomfortable.

I could never tell Ellis that, but I definitely see Duke's point now.

Of course Keith doesn't want Ellis joking around about Keith and Leila finding Leon in a dumpster, especially not with Duke and Naomi standing right there holding Amelia.

Ellis has no idea how inappropriate that sounds because he doesn't remember how Duke and Naomi got Amelia in the first place.

Keith also doesn't want Ellis joking around about Keith accidentally dropping his baby son on his head. I wince when I remember it—as if Keith Brewer would ever let anything happen to Leon. Please.

I struggle to come up with a way to explain it to Ellis in a way that will make sense to him without hurting his feelings, but a lot of other things Duke said come back to haunt me, too.

The longer this goes on, the longer I spend time with Ellis as his old, joking, fun-loving self, the more I understand why Duke said Ellis was changing for the better when he got all quiet and serious.

He understood then. He understood all about everything. He became more sensitive, more compassionate, more attentive, and more caring.

He doesn't even understand how he changed because he doesn't remember it.

He notices my silence and shoots me another sharp look. "What? Don't tell me I really did have something to do with John's death."

"No, you didn't. I already told you what happened. You can ask anyone here if you don't believe me."

He looks away. "I'm not going to ask anyone that. They're already touchy enough."

"That's what I mean. They're touchy for a reason. We all are. That's the way things are around here now. Everyone is touchy about it, but it's okay because we all understand why we're touchy." I open my mouth to say something else and stop myself.

I don't want to tell him that he's the only one who isn't touchy because he's the only person here who didn't go through it with us—or doesn't remember going through it with us.

The fact that he wants to act like John never died is somehow so deeply offensive. I don't dare tell him that.

I don't get a chance to because, right at that moment, as if out of a forgotten dimension of time, Keith and Danny both come up to the parking lot to get stuff out of their cars.

Keith is still holding Leon on his shoulder and has to do everything one-handed. He arches an eyebrow at me and Ellis. "Are you two okay?"

"We're fine," I reply.

Ellis pushes himself off the fender and spins around to confront them. "Actually, no, we aren't. I want to talk to you two. What is your problem with me? You've been holding me at arm's length ever since I got out of the hospital and you just told me to keep my mouth shut, Keith. What's going on?"

Keith closes up his face into a solid wall of ice the way he does when something is really bothering him. He slams his trunk extra hard and then pats Leon on the back when the noise startles the baby.

Danny breaks the awkward silence. "I guess the problem is that none of us knows how to deal with you now, man. You're so different."

"I'm not different!" Ellis counters. "I'm back to the way I was before! You're all the ones who are different. Jessie says you don't blame me for John's death....."

"We don't," Danny replies. "We never did. You were the one who blamed yourself for John's death even when we tried to talk you out of it."

"Well, I don't blame myself for his death now!" Ellis points out. "You should be happy that I don't blame myself anymore, but you're the ones who are all acting weird around me."

"No one blames you for John's death," Keith growls. "That doesn't mean we want you constantly joking about."

Ellis blanches again. "I wasn't making a joke about that, man. I would never make a joke about that."

"But you would make a joke out of everything else that happens to fall out of your mouth," Keith snaps and immediately softens his tone. "The person you were—the person who blamed himself—you were the one who suffered the worst from this—even more than me and Danny—and now you don't even remember that it happened. You don't know what it was like to be there and watch it happen—or what we had to go through afterward. You joking around the way you do almost feels like an insult to John's memory. His death brought us closer together because we were all there. We all went through it—and we all went through the aftermath together. We had to lean on each other to get through it—and so did you. It brought us closer to you, too, but you don't remember that, either, do you? We all cared about you because John's death touched you the way it touched us. It doesn't touch you now. You don't even know it happened except that someone told you about it. You're an outsider, man. You're the one person here who doesn't understand." He turns away. "We tried a million times to bring you back, but you wouldn't listen. I would have done anything to take that burden off your shoulders, but now I'm really starting to wish you were still like that."

He bends down, picks up the bag he took out of the trunk, and walks off with it down the beach. He leaves Ellis speechless.

Chapter 11: Ellis

I pull up in front of Jessie's apartment building and switch off the motor.

I should take this moment to make out with her before she goes back inside, but I can't stop thinking about what Keith said.

I'm an outsider. I'm not a member of their crew because I didn't go through John's death with them.

I understand what he means, but how am I supposed to fix that? It isn't my fault I can't remember John's death.

I don't even want to remember John's death. It sounds horrific.

Why would I want to remember something that completely ruined all our lives, especially mine? I don't want my life ruined. I don't want to go back to that.

Wouldn't it be worth it to go back to that if I got the crew back?

In answer to my question, Jessie slips her hand into mine. She doesn't ask if I'm okay because she can see that I'm not.

I really am a lucky bastard to have a woman like this sitting next to me. She's always been unbelievably kind to me.

We've always been close. I just never knew how close until this happened.

I never would have believed she could be so caring and affectionate toward me—because I never had any problems bad enough that I needed her to act caring and affection toward me.

I lived a charmed life before. I never really had any problems at all.

Maybe that's the problem. I was a dopey kid who didn't understand anything, including myself.

She squeezes my hand and I squeeze back, but I can't look at her. I stare through the windshield at the apartment building instead.

She's one of the crew—the crew I'm not a part of anymore. She's one of the people who understands—one of the people on the inside. She was there. She went through it with them.

She understands what to say and when to say it without upsetting anyone.

I don't even know how to talk to her anymore. Is this what happened to me before? Is this how I just stopped talking completely—because I didn't want to offend anyone?

They don't say that. They say I blamed myself—and Keith said me going silent actually brought me closer to them. How does that even work if my silence bothered them all so much?

How can Keith say that John's death doesn't touch me? How can anyone who knew John Brewer not be touched by his death?

Jessie breaks me out of my trance. "I'm going to go inside. Are you going to be okay?"

I glance at her, and as soon as we make eye contact, I can't look away. I have to look at her and acknowledge her. I have to be with her here right in this moment. Being near her is too important.

"Yeah, I'll be fine," I mumble. "I just have a lot on my mind."

"That's a good thing. That's the first step."

I find myself studying her. "You agree with him, don't you—about me being an outsider because I didn't go through it? You agree with him that I don't understand."

She shrugs and looks away. "You had to hear it from someone. I can't think of anyone better for you to hear it from than him. I don't think you would have been able to hear it from me."

I stiffen and compress my lips. "Would you want me to go back to being like that even if it meant we couldn't be together?"

She winces. "I wouldn't want you to go back to being like that because I couldn't stand to see you suffer over something that wasn't your fault. I just want what's best for you—and I don't even know what that is right now."

"You're what's best for me. I want to be with you. You said I pushed you away when I was like that. I wouldn't want to go back to that."

"I wouldn't want you to push me away, but I also don't want you to be someone that is missing such a big, important part of who you really are. You changed a lot in the last year—and I don't mean the part about you not talking or coming to the barbecues. Everything about you changed."

"How?" I ask.

"You became more caring, more considerate, more helpful...."

"I still care about you and the crew as much as I ever did. You can't tell me I stopped caring."

"I don't mean that. I can't exactly explain it because I don't understand it, but Keith is right. It brought us all closer together, including you. You were still one of us even when you isolated yourself. You were more one of us then than....."

She trails off. She doesn't have to say the rest because I hear it in her silence.

She means I was more one of them when I was silent than I am now.

Everything Keith said was true. This is why Keith Brewer is the man. He can say things like this to people and we have no choice but to listen.

I try to look away again and she notices. She squeezes my hand and dives in to kiss me on the cheek. "I'll see you at work tomorrow. I had a really nice time with you. Don't worry. This will all work out one way or the other. Don't let it bother you too much."

She doesn't wait for me to open her door for her before she slips out of the truck, dashes across the parking lot to her apartment building, and vanishes inside.

I sit there staring after her for a minute just trying to get my thoughts into some kind of order. I don't even know what or how to think about any of this anymore.

I drive back to my place and spend way too long just looking around staring at everything.

I was apparently really conscientious about my nutrition, workouts, sleep, and work schedule before this happened, but I can't get interested in any of that now.

I can't bring myself to do much of anything, so I just veg out in front of the TV for the rest of the evening. It's the only way I can take my mind off what Keith said.

I don't see how I can change anything that he and Danny seem to think is wrong with me—except if I stop joking around.

I can't make myself one of the crew. If remembering John's death is the price of admission, then I'm stuck out in the cold.

I'm not even sure if I should go to work tomorrow after what he said, but I'm already rostered, so I have to go.

The thought of seeing Jessie again makes the decision for me. She's the one good thing coming out of all of this.

I stay up way too late watching reruns of *Game of Thrones* and eventually crash.

My alarm wakes me up. I take a shower and go to the firehouse the way I usually do.

I keep things businesslike while we do our checks. I get through the morning without anyone telling me to keep my mouth shut or giving me any dirty looks or acting weird around me.

We're just about to go upstairs to the breakroom when we get a call. Keith, Billy, Danny, Caleb, and I climb into the rescue truck with Josh and Allison. Jessie is on the ladder truck today.

"We got trembling in a building downtown!" Billy reads off the computer.

"Trembling!" Danny exclaims. "We don't get earthquakes in this part of the country."

"Take it up with the manager," Billy tells him. "The stairwells are unstable with forty people trapped on one of the upper floors. Another fifteen trapped in an elevator. Power is out to the whole building."

"Yikes!" Keith mutters.

Duke passes us in his support pickup just then. He meets us at the scene.

The Police control another one hundred people standing around in the parking lot outside the affected building.

"No injuries out here!" Police Chief Jim Walker tells us. "At this point, it's all extrication. We have a crane on the way over to get the people off the upper floors, but we don't even know where they are."

"We'll take it from here." Duke turns to the rest of us. "There are four stairwells at the outer building corners. Split up into teams and check every stairwell to see how stable they are. If you find one that is still intact, use it to get up there and locate the people. The crane will come to this side of the building, so bring everyone over here and signal us so we can get everyone down. The city engineers are coming over to check the foundations and find out what caused the rumbling. They'll take a look at the elevator and figure out what we need to do about that so we can evacuate safely."

We divide up by truck. Keith, Josh, Danny, and I go to one of the stairwells. Billy, Caleb, and Allison go to the other stairwell on the south side.

The ladder truck crew splits up, too, with Chris and Jessie each going with a different team.

Keith, Danny, Josh, and I enter our stairwell through the outer emergency exit door on the ground floor.

Keith peers up the stairwell. "Everything looks stable here. Let's go."

We start climbing. All four of us make sure to check, double-check, and study all the walls on our way up.

We make it to the tenth floor before Duke contacts Keith on the radio. "The building manager says the only people unaccounted for work on the twentieth floor. Check there first."

"You got it. If the other teams need to move around, the southeast stairwell looks intact."

"The northwest stairwell has collapsed, so stay away from that side of the building," Duke tells us. "The engineers are here so I'm pulling back one of the ladder truck teams to help with the elevator."

Chapter 12: Ellis

J osh, Keith, Danny, and I make much better progress to the twentieth floor.

We see the problem right away when we leave the stairwell. A bunch of walls have broken down for some reason. I don't try to understand it.

"Is anyone here?!" Keith yells out. "We're from the Fire Department! We're here to help get you out! Call out if you can hear me!"

A dozen voices answer him from farther up the corridor.

We follow the sound to an office. A mountain of caved-in debris blocks the entrance doorway. No one can get in or out.

"Help us!" someone calls from inside. "We're stuck in here!"

"We're right outside the room!" Keith yells through the blockage. "Just sit tight! We're going to get you out!"

"The question is how we're going to get them out," Danny remarks.

"These walls don't look too thick," I point out. "We can chop through one of the side rooms with our axes."

Keith shrugs. "Good idea. Let's go."

We go into the first room on the left and discover that a big glass window connecting this room to the office with the people inside it. They must have panicked and didn't think to break the glass.

The trapped people rush the window as soon as they see us. They pound on the glass.

Keith waves them away and points to the other side of the room. It takes a long time for them to calm down enough to do what he says.

He finally stands back, smashes his axe through the glass, and shatters the window.

We help everyone climb out. Keith nods at me. "Go check on the other side of the building and see if the crane is there."

"Why not just take them down the stairs?" Danny asks.

Almost as if his words make it happen, a deep rumble shakes the building right them.

The trapped people all scream and hit the floor. They hold onto the carpet for protection, but the tremor stops almost immediately.

Keith, Danny, Josh, and I exchange glances and look at the ceiling before Keith points at me. "Go. Go now."

I hustle away to the other side of the floor. Josh starts checking the patients for injuries.

I have to clamber over broken walls and piles of debris to get to the windows facing the street side of the building.

The crane is there with its bucket extended as far as it will reach, but it doesn't come up as high as this floor.

I open the window and wave to Chief Walker on the ground. Then I contact Duke on the radio. "We found everyone, but the crane isn't long enough," I tell him. "We'll have to take the stairs."

"You can't," he tells me. "The lower levels are destabilizing. Stay where you are until we bring in a bigger crane."

I go back and tell Keith what's going on. He makes a face. "This is nuts."

He gets busy taking everyone back to the other side of the building. We have to stand around and wait for the first crane to leave, the second one to arrive, and for the operator to set up his outriggers.

The bucket finally rises slowly toward our window. It parks against the side of the building and Keith loads Josh into the bucket with seven of the employees.

They all start sobbing hysterically when the bucket drifts away from the wall to descend toward the ground.

The bucket gets ten feet away from the window when another dangerous shudder goes through the floor and walls. The sound of breaking glass comes from somewhere behind us.

None of the rest of us say anything, but we're all thinking the same thing. We gotta get out of here.

The bucket takes way too long to lower to the ground. Josh helps the employees out and then the bucket starts rising again. Everything takes an age.

Danny gets into the bucket with the second group of passengers. That leaves me, Keith, and three others waiting for doomsday.

I can't watch the bucket sink toward the ground. Keith is already standing there watching everything like the hawk he is. He'll tell me if anything happens.

I turn away and try to smile at the last three employees. "Don't worry," I tell them. "Everything is gonna be fine."

"Did everyone else make it out of the building?" a portly, balding man in a dark blue suit asks me.

"There are a few people still trapped in the elevator, but the city engineers are working on it with another crew from the Fire Department. We would have heard if the building was in any danger."

I don't know if my comments put the guy at ease, but I can only try.

The bucket comes back. Keith climbs on and holds out his hands. "Come on over and we'll take you down. Come on. It's fine. You're almost there."

The other three employees are a young woman with long brown hair, the portly guy I was just talking to, and another older guy with a thick ruff of frizzy white hair surrounding his head.

The two men stand back to let the woman get into the bucket first. I offer her my hand to steady herself when she climbs over the windowsill.

She shrieks when she sees how high off the ground she is. Then Keith catches her as soon as she topples into the bucket.

I help the old man to climb in and then both Keith and I have to steady the portly guy. His weight makes it difficult for him to balance on the windowsill and then he steps on the woman when he does finally get into the bucket.

Keith waves me forward. "Come on, Ellis."

I swing my leg over the windowsill, but right then, another deep crack goes through the building.

I don't notice the building move that much, but it must have. The wall and the windowsill bump the crane bucket and it drifts five feet away from the window.

I'm still sitting there with my leg hanging over the side. At first, I think the crane operator will just move the bucket closer to the window so I can get in.

He must not realize what happened because he starts to lower the bucket even while Keith is still standing there with his hand out to help me.

"Hold tight!" he yells up at me. "We'll be right back to get you!"

I shrug at nothing and pull my leg back in. Now I have nothing to do but wait.

The instant I bring my leg inside, another deep shudder hits the building—and this one doesn't stop. It rumbles the floor and then the whole building jostles hard enough to knock me off my feet.

I sprawl and the tremor shatters the windows behind me. I duck under my arms as broken glass rains all over my helmet and turnouts.

At the same instant, my radio crackles in my ear. "Pull out!" Duke yells. "Get out of the building by any means necessary! The upper floors are destabilizing!"

I'm the only person on the upper floors. The only way out is the southwest stairwell and I don't even know if that is still intact.

I have to chance it. The crane operator won't be able to send the bucket back for me if the building is this unstable.

Duke didn't say the lower floors were destabilizing. Maybe, if I get low enough, I'll be able to find a way out.

I scramble to my feet, but continuous shakes and jostling impacts keep hurling me sideways. I crash into the walls and debris keeps showering on my head everywhere I go.

I charge back to the stairwell. I don't take the time to check how stable or intact it is. I don't really care. This is my only way out of the building. I have to take my chances or die in here.

I blunder onto the first landing. Hunks of concrete and other random crap hurtles past me down the stairwell, deflects off the walls and stairs, and some of it hits me.

I huddle under my arms and just keep on running. I pound down the stairs as well as I can in between more concussions that throw me from side to side.

One of them knocks me down the stairs and I roll to the next landing. I'm just scrambling to get to my feet again when a catastrophic impact hits the building.

The whole stairwell dissolves in front of me, falls away into nothing, and leaves a yawning chasm in front of me. I won't be able to get out that way—if I can get out at all.

A matching rockfall of boulders and twisted re-bar plunges down the stairwell from above me. I catch one glimpse before it buries me under a mountain of rubble and I dive out of the way just in time.

I escape through the only route left—back inside the building. I dive through the stairwell door and take off running. I don't even care where I'm going.

I can only think one thing. I have to take refuge at the center of the building. The stairwells are located at the outer corners.

Whatever is causing this building to collapse must be working its way from the outside to the inside. So the building interior will be the safest—I hope.

I charge around a corner not thinking too much about where the hell I am and I almost collide with Duke. He and the city engineers gather around the elevator bay on this floor. The doors stand open while they all peer through the hole at something down the shaft.

I stagger to a halt when my addled brain realizes where I am and why. Duke looks up at me and his eyes widen. "What are you doing here? You should have gotten out with the crane."

I open my mouth, but my voice doesn't seem to connect up with any rational thought.

I wave behind me while I try to catch my breath. "The stairs.....they're gone....."

His features harden. "Stay here. We'll have to use the crane...but we gotta get these people out first."

He bends over to look down the shaft. The engineers have set up a winch with a cable dropping down to the elevator. The car seems to be stuck between floors.

I look over Duke's shoulder to see what's happening. My stomach drops when I look through the open elevator ceiling hatch. Jessie kneels on the floor inside the elevator.

"What's the situation?" Duke calls down.

"We have three critical patients who need extrication," she calls back. "Everyone else is all right! You can take them first....but I'll need backboards and C-spine immobilization to get the rest of these pati ents....and another pair of hands would help a lot."

"We don't have any immobilization equipment and I don't dare to let another crew enter the building to bring it to us. We'll just have to extricate the patients the way they are and immobilize them afterward. Ellis is here. I'll send him down." Duke turns to me. "You're going in, s on."

He gets on the radio and calls down to the crane to tell the operator where we are. The engineers get hold of me and strap me up with a belaying harness over my turnouts.

I nearly have an aneurysm when I lean back over the elevator shaft and the engineers lower me toward the ceiling hatch. It looks so small from here.

Jessie watches me in between attending to her patients. I hear her talking to the other employees to reassure them.

I land on top of the elevator, drop through the hole, shimmy out of the harness, and start fitting it to the first person nearest to me.

I see what Jessie means. The critical patients sprawl on the floor. They don't leave enough room for the rest of these people to stand inside the elevator.

I want to clear as many people out of here as I can to leave room for Jessie to work.

I don't see her starting IVs, intubating, or treating the critical patients in any way. I'm too busy to ask myself why not.

I put the harness on another middle-aged lady first. She has to hitch her skirts up around her waist so the harness fits. She whimpers when we all see her in her underwear.

"Your life is more important than this," I tell her. "No one cares what you look like as long as you make it out of here in one piece. Got it?"

She nods at me fast, but she's already bordering on hysterical. I clip the cable to her harness and yell through the hole. "Take it up!"

I steer her through the hole and the engineers pull her up.

The employees burst into screams each time another tremor hits the building. I don't blame them. The noise and shuddering impacts are really getting on my nerves.

We have to work fast, but we can't do anything but wait for the engineers to lift everyone out and then lower the cable back down to me.

I work as fast as I can and get the last employees out. Then Jessie and I have to work together to load up the critical patients.

The engineers send down full-body harnesses for them. The patients' arms, legs, and heads flop. I have to angle them into the right position so they don't bump into the ceiling hatch.

Duke and the engineers pull the last patient onto the floor and the engineers start lowering the harness for me and Jessie.

"You go first," I tell her.

She bursts into a smile and then pulls me away from the hole. She attacks me against the wall and kisses me hard, but she does it where Duke and the others can't see us.

The harness falls through the hole and we get back to business when I bend down to help her step into the harness loops.

I strap it around her and smile at her, but I have to get serious when I straighten up to call out to the engineers. We're almost out of here. We're almost safe.

"Take it up!" I yell.

The cable tightens and lifts Jessie's feet off the floor. She smiles down at me and then looks up to guide herself through the hole.

She raises her arms to the rim and pulls her head through it. At that moment, a shivering boom strikes the building from somewhere and a crack like a gunshot goes off somewhere.

Jessie plummets back inside the elevator. I barely get my arms up in time to break her fall before gravity yanks the elevator away and sends it plunging down the shaft.

Jessie's weight falls against me and we both buckle to the floor. The elevator is falling too fast for either of us to get up—and then it smashes down on a hard surface with a bone-crushing impact.

Chapter 13: Jessie

I blink dust out of my eyes and try to see in the dark, but not a hint of light penetrates the elevator.

I become aware of Ellis lying next to me with his arms around me. He coughs once. "Are you all right, sweetie?" he chokes.

"I'm fine...." I struggle to sit up.

I have to break his grip and it takes him an extra minute to relax before he pries himself away from me. He held me against himself when the elevator crashed.

"Are you all right?" I ask. "Did you get hurt?"

"I'm fine." He pulls away and sits up. "Hold on a second. I have a flashlight."

I hear him unfasten his turnouts and then he switches on a flashlight. It brightens up the elevator—as much as it can be brightened.

He shines the light around and sighs. "I guess we're here now. The cable must have broken." He grins at me. "Now you're stuck with only me for company. Is this your idea of Heaven or what?"

I snort at him. "Keep telling yourself that, Casanova. I just hope the building doesn't collapse on top of us and trap us here forever."

He brings his face closer to me and positions the flashlight right under his chin. The light shines up his face and casts ghostly circles around his eyes, nose, and cheekbones to make him look scary.

"MMwwwaaaaahhhhaaaahhhhaaaa!" he chortles. "I come to suck your blooooooood!"

I laugh and push him away. "Cut it out! You're going to waste your flashlight batteries."

He snickers and pushes himself to his feet. "I'm going to climb up there and see where we are. There might be an access ladder we can use to get out of here."

He strips off his turnouts, kicks off his heavy protective pants and boots, and lays them aside along with his helmet. He's wearing his normal uniform underneath.

He sticks the end of his flashlight in his mouth to hold it, takes a position right underneath the ceiling hatch, jumps, catches the rim, and pulls himself up there.

He struggles through the hole, sits on the top of the elevator, and shines his flashlight in all directions.

"The good news is that it doesn't sound like the building is shaking anymore," he calls down. "It sounds quiet."

"So what's the bad news?" I ask.

"I don't see any emergency access ladder.....no, wait. There it is, but fallen debris is blocking it. We won't be able to get out that way."

Just then, my radio crackles. "Ellis—Jessie!" Duke calls. "Can you hear me?!"

I grab my radio. "We're here! We're both all right. We're at the bottom of the elevator shaft trapped in the elevator, but we're both all right."

"Just hang on!" Duke tells me. "We're coming to get you out, but it might take a while. We're working on it as fast as we can."

"Don't worry about us," I tell him. "We're safe here for now."

"Great. The engineers are working on a way to access the elevator shaft from one of the stable floors.....except that there aren't any stable floors."

I groan, but I make sure not to do it over the radio. "We aren't going anywhere. We'll just take a long lunch here until you come and get us."

He chuckles through the speaker. "Save some tuna salad for me."

We hang up and Ellis jumps down. "I should turn this off in case we need it later."

"We should sit down and conserve our energy. We don't know how long we'll be stuck in here."

We both sit down against the wall and he switches off his flashlight.

We sit in silence for a minute before Ellis breaks it. "Did you hear the one about the dog who dressed up as a marshmallow for Halloween?"

I make a face even though he can't see me in the dark. "You aren't going to spend our time down here making jokes, are you?"

He changes his tone instantly. "Does it really bother you that much? You never said. You should have told me if I was being so annoying."

"It isn't that." I take his hand in the dark. He feels good sitting here next to me. "Whatever this is that's going on between us, I don't want it to be another joke."

"It isn't," he breathes. "I was just trying to help you get through it.....you know....by keeping the mood light."

"The mood doesn't always need to be light," I tell him. "Especially not between us."

Out of nowhere, his hand slides into my hair and he pulls me against his mouth. His hot breath sizzles on my cheeks and lips when he kisses me.

"I don't want the mood to be light between us," he whispers and falls on my mouth to stop me from answering.

He kisses me for a long time before he breaks away. He doesn't start joking around again.

We go back to sitting in silence. I don't know how to approach this situation with him. We can't even see each other.

It's eerie not being able to look into his eyes even though I know what he looks like.

"You're very special to me," he murmurs after a while. "I would never want to do anything to jeopardize what we have."

"You're very special to me, too," I tell him and then hesitate. "What do we have? What is this? What are we doing?"

He doesn't answer for a minute. What is he thinking? I can't tell when I can't see him.

I probably wouldn't be able to tell even if I could see him.

I'm just giving up on him saying anything when he murmurs, "Take off your turnouts and come sit on my lap. I want to feel you."

I push myself onto my knees and climb out of my turnouts. I'm not sure where to go or how to position myself, but he answers that question for me by taking hold of me before I get there.

He rotates me backward and steers me to sit down sideways on his lap. His arms fold around me and he draws me into a close embrace.

His fingers trail through my hair and explore my face in the dark.

"How I felt about you was always serious," he murmurs. "I never thought of our friendship as a joke."

"Why didn't you tell me? Why didn't you tell me you wanted to make it serious? You always seemed satisfied to leave it the way it was. We probably never would have been anything more than friends if John hadn't gotten killed."

"Maybe I thought you didn't want me to take it any further....or maybe I didn't think I needed to take it any further. Maybe it was too familiar and comfortable the way it was."

"What would you have done if I got with another guy? Then you would have backed off and faded into the background while I built a life with someone else."

"You're right," he murmurs. "I probably wouldn't have tried to intervene then. I guess it's a good thing that we're here now. I can tell you how I feel about you and show you that I want more."

"When did you realize you wanted to change things between us? If you woke up in the hospital thinking it was a year ago, you would have felt the same way about me."

His body moves like he's looking over at me. "I don't know what happened, but I felt it as soon as you walked into the hospital room to visit me with the crew. I noticed you in the group right away. I felt like you shouldn't be standing over there on the side so far away from me. I wanted you right next to me, sitting on the edge of the bed, and even lying down next to me with your arms around me. I wanted everyone else to leave so we could be alone together and I could tell you how much you mean to me. I understood why you were standing over there on the side, but it felt all wrong and I knew I wanted to change it." He hesitates again. "Why do you want to know that?"

"Maybe the car accident did something to you. I mean, we know it made you lose your memory, but maybe it changed things in other ways. Maybe it changed the part of your personality that made you think of me as a friend."

"I don't know, but I'm glad it did. I'm glad we're here like this now. I don't want it to go back to the way it was." He squeezes me tighter against him. "You feel too good like this."

I don't know what to say to that. He's been acting so differently lately—even so much more differently than he acted a year ago. I can't put that down to his memory loss or even a head injury.

I don't know how much longer he'll stay like this. He could wake up tomorrow morning and remember John's death—and remember why he never asked me out before.

I don't even know if this is the real Ellis—but I want to take advantage of this moment while I can. I don't want to let it pass without at least appreciating all that he is.

His hand falls on my hip when he hugs me. Does he even realize how suggestive this position is?

He might never take it any further. He might want more from me, but his feelings still seem so innocent even if they aren't platonic anymore.

I wait, but he doesn't even try to kiss me again. Will he ever take it further?

Maybe he doesn't think he can. Maybe he doesn't think he can cross the line with me and still respect me afterward.

I'll never find a better time than now to find out.

I wait one more moment just to make sure he doesn't plan to do anything himself.

Then I cast my doubts aside, pivot on his lap, and throw my other leg over him to straddle his hips.

He doesn't move for a second. He freezes under me.

I could kiss him right now and let the heat build between us, but I want to do this another way.

The world stops when I lay my hands on his chest. His muscles tense to a wall of iron when I feel him through his T-shirt.

His heart pounds through his sternum. He's bigger and stronger than he's ever been in all the time I've known him.

The air between us charges with silent potential. He knows what I'm doing.

I caress down his T-shirt to his stomach, take hold of his shirt, and lift it to pull it off.

He helps guide it over his own head and sits back in front of me shirtless.

My hands trace the clefts of his chest and stomach. His breath catches in his nostrils. He doesn't make any other sound. He doesn't move. He sits unnaturally still and lets me touch him.

I peel my T-shirt off, grab his wrists, and raise his hands to touch me in my bra. His hands and body come alive when his warm palms graze my bare skin.

He massages my breasts until I moan. I can't keep away from him like this.

I fall on him and kiss his chest and neck in big, hot, wet, mouthfuls. He gasps through his teeth and doesn't stop touching me when I crawl all over him.

His hands glide up my arms to my neck and he hugs my head into his chest when I mouth down to his stomach.

His other hand comes to rest on my back and then he pulls down my bra straps.

I whimper in delight when he lifts me up, unclips my bra, and his hungry mouth takes hold of my nipples one after another.

His mouth sends fireworks rocketing through me when he sucks them in. His hands range all over me and his package swells to bursting inside his pants.

I ride down on his bulge, and just as fast, he tears away and dives for my mouth. He kisses me in raving hunger and tries to tear his pants open.

I have to stand up to take my pants and boots off. I can't see him at all, so he can't see me, either.

His heat explodes my mind apart when I lower myself into a straddle and feel his naked hardness underneath me.

I don't have a plan for this part of the act, but he sure seems to. He grabs me and pulls me onto his shaft fast enough to make me scream. Before I know what hit me, he swivels onto his knees with me impaled on his shaft.

I arch back into his thrusts, but he's already bending over and angling me down on top of it while he drills into me from below.

My thighs fall around him and he propels me into a screaming climax that blows my whole world to smithereens.

I scream out. If anyone is in this building, they'll hear me bursting into one reeling climax after another as he plows me deep and true.

He plunges his face into my neck and then gnaws down to my chest. I can't feel anything but this avalanche of bliss as he unloads into me and searing heat lights me up from the inside.

Chapter 14: Ellis

My eyes snap open in the dark. Just for a second, I think I had a dream about doing it with Jessie. Mmmm, what a hot, delicious, succulent dream it was, too.

It wasn't a dream, though. I really did it with her.

She wanted me to. She started it.

Now she sits next to me on the elevator floor with her clothes back on—and I have my clothes back on.

Doing it with her like that doesn't satisfy me at all. I want to see her. I want to lock her in my basement and make her writhe and scream for a week—or longer, preferably.

I want to consume every part of her. I want to keep going until neither of us can keep going any longer.

Maybe that little quickie is all she wants. Even that seems innocent—almost like we're still friends. I don't want that.

I don't dare to tell her how much I want. I would probably scare her into running away completely.

I have to take it slow and easy. I have to be gentle with her. I wouldn't want to hurt her.

Even her sitting right next to me in the dark is too far away, but I can't take it further—not now.

We could get rescued any second now. I wouldn't want Duke or anyone else to find us down here with our clothes off in some uncompromising position.

I might think it was worth it to do that, but I wouldn't want to embarrass her. I care about her too much.

I try to think about how to proceed with her, but I don't even know when we're going to get out of here.

I make a conscious decision not to check my watch. I have to push the button to switch on the face illumination to see the time. It's only seven o'clock in the morning. We've been down here less than twenty-four hours. Things could get a lot worse.

We could die of dehydration in this elevator before someone rescues us.

That probably won't happen. Duke and the crew are out there working on this right now.

I just wish I could think of something to say to Jessie—something other than filling the airwaves with some stupid joke.

I don't seem to be able to say anything after I just did it with her. Doing it with her better not ruin our relationship—or our friendship. I'm going to be furious if it does.

Out of nowhere, she murmurs in the dark, "What do you want to talk about?"

"I'm not sure," I tell her. "Maybe you could tell me something else that happened in the last year—something that doesn't involve anyone I know or care about getting shot, killed, or attacked by a raving psychopath."

"Well.....Josh and Chris got married.....and Duke and Naomi got married.....and then they adopted Amelia....."

"Adopted!" I spin around. "Why did they adopt?"

She turns to face me in the dark. "You don't remember. Naomi had a day off work. She was at the mall when a woman went into labor. Naomi helped her give birth...and a few days later, the woman showed up at the firehouse and surrendered the baby to Duke. He and Naomi kept her."

"That's amazing!" I breathe. "What else happened?"

"Brooke and Billy got married, too. I forgot to mention them."

"Wow. I never thought he would settle down with anyone. He always comes across as such a hard-ass."

I realize where this conversation is going. I'm only talking and asking and finding out how much everyone has changed in the last year.

I need to change the subject, but right then, she slips her hand into mine. "I really like you," she murmurs. "I like you a lot."

"I like you, too, sweetie." I gather my resolve to say the next part. "I love you—and not just as a friend. I want us to have something real—something that lasts."

"How can we when we don't even know who or what you're going to be tomorrow?"

"You said you liked me even when I was the other way."

"I did, but you don't remember if you liked me that way. You might change your mind if you got your memory back."

"The first step is to get out of this elevator. After that, we'll just have to go ahead as if I'm going to stay like this."

She lowers her voice a little more. "I don't know if I can do that. I don't know if I can invest in someone who would just leave me at the drop of a hat."

"I would never leave you! I couldn't do that!"

"You don't even know if you would—or if you could. You don't remember."

I don't know what to say. I want to tell myself and her that I'm certain I wouldn't, but she's right.

"I wish I could remember," I tell her. "There's this wall between me and all of that. I wish I could remember how I felt about you then."

"If you remembered that, you would have to remember John. Maybe you never lost your memory at all. Maybe you're blocking it out so you don't have to live with all the guilt and pain."

I look away even though she can't see me. I don't want to think about that.

I don't want to remember John dying. I want to remember him alive and strong and in charge of everything.

I want to keep living under the illusion that he's still out there somewhere even if I can't see him right now. My world doesn't make sense without that.

I turn my head toward her. I would give anything to see her eyes right now.

I can barely speak above a whisper. "Would you ever do it with me again? Was that just a one-time thing?"

She keeps her voice to a low murmur, too. "I would do it with you again. I would do it with you a lot. You seem to think I'm a lot more innocent than I am."

I don't know what to think or say to that, either, but it lights my insides on fire. Holy Christ, I want her!

I want to do it with her again right now, but right at that moment, we hear a slam above us and then a light flickers through the darkness outside the ceiling hatch.

"Jessie—Ellis!" Duke calls. "Are you down there?"

Jessie and I scramble to our feet. "We're here!" we both yell. "We're down here!"

"Hold on!" he calls back. "We're coming to get you out!"

Jessie squeals, dives for me, and throws her arms around my neck. We can see more as dozens of lights stream down the elevator shaft from above.

We break apart both laughing. The noise up there escalates with dozens of voices echoing down the shaft. I recognize the firehouse guys talking to the engineers.

Jessie and I hug again. I want to kiss her, but not in front of the crew.

We both hustle around the elevator putting our turnouts back on. We finish just as Billy drops into the shaft on the end of another cable.

He lands on the elevator roof and peers at us through the hole. "You two okay?" he asks. "Does either of you need medical attention?"

"We're fine!" I yell back. "Just get us the hell out of here!"

He bursts into a grin and starts tearing off his harness. "Put this on."

He lowers the cable through the hole and I help Jessie put on the harness. I steer her through the hole and Billy guides her clear so the engineers can pull her up.

I almost want to cry when she vanishes into the darkness and I hear all the rest of the crew talking to her up there.

Then it's my turn. Billy grins at me and claps me on the shoulder when the cable lifts me past him.

The whole crew pulls me to safety and they all surround me talking at once. Someone else takes my harness off and the crew escorts me and Jessie out of the building.

We wind up riding back to the firehouse in separate trucks the same way we got here.

No one will stop talking about all the work they've been doing to find a safe way into the building so they could set up another winch to get into the elevator shaft.

"What did you and Jessie do the whole time you were down there?" Caleb asks.

"We just talked....."

"Don't lie," Keith teases. "You killed her with terrible jokes the whole time, didn't you?"

"You'll be proud of me. I didn't tell one joke the whole time."

"I don't believe you," Danny counters.

"I shone the flashlight under my face to make myself look like Dracula—and I said I would suck her blood." The guys laugh. "Then I had to turn off the flashlight to conserve the batteries. I guess neither of us felt like joking around after that."

The crew talks and asks me more questions, but I don't really feel like talking. I'll never tell what really happened in that elevator. That's just between me and Jessie.

We get back to the firehouse by eleven o'clock in the morning and get a call ten minutes later. It's the middle of the shift and Jessie and I are both rostered to work today.

No one mentions us taking the rest of the day off. She and I don't mention it, either, so we wind up going with the crew to deal with the situation.

The crew winds up in the breakroom afterward. I open the fridge. "I'm starving—and thirsty."

"There's some leftover spareribs in there from the last barbecue," Sophie tells me. "And there's a bottle of lemonade in the door."

"Yeah, that's perfect!" I pull everything out of the fridge and yell over my shoulder to Jessie across the room. "Do you want some, sweetie?"

"Yeah, great!" she calls back.

I put the ribs in the microwave and pour the lemonade into glasses for both of us. I bump Caleb's shoulder when I bring the two plates to the table. "Stand aside, kind Sir. The savages are about to engage in their annual cannibal feast."

He laughs and the rest of the crew shoots rude remarks back and forth when Jessie and I sit down at the table to gorge ourselves.

She takes the first bite and rolls her eyes in ecstasy. "Oh, my God! I'm going to die!"

I guzzle down a big mouthful of lemonade. "Just make sure you die with a full stomach."

"You're gonna have to take those macros off the rest of the week at the rate you're going," Danny tells me.

"I don't care if this is the last meal I eat for a month." I take a huge bite of my ribs and get the sauce all over my face.

Chris laughs at me. "Take a bath in it."

"I think I will." I wipe my face, but right at that moment, we get another call.

Jessie and I get swept up in it and go out with the rest of the crew again. We don't make it back to the firehouse until it's time for both of us to go off shift.

I catch up with her in the locker room as we're both packing up. She grins at me across the room. "Are you going to take your ribs home with you?"

I sidle over to her and lean my shoulder against the lockers. "Why don't you let me take you out to dinner tonight? We can do it the right way."

She brightens up and smiles at me. "That would be great. I would love that."

I dart in and kiss her. "I'll pick you up at seven, okay?"

She blushes. "I can't wait."

I would like nothing better than to put my arms around her and kiss her long and deep right here in the locker room. I would really like to feel her legs wrapped around my waist and feel her hair falling over my face, but that will have to wait.

Chapter 15: Jessie

I get out of the shower and stand in front of my closet for a long time. I have to decide what to wear on my dinner date with Ellis.

I should have gotten more information from him about where we're going.

He might decide to take me to a rib joint where we can rut around in squalor and get sauce all over ourselves the way we did in the breakroom.

Or he might decide to go somewhere nicer. I should have asked to find out.

I'll have to split the difference and hope I'm not too overdressed or underdressed.

I could wear the little black dress I wore to the fun park, but that would be overkill for a feed of ribs, mashed potatoes, and fries dripping with ketchup.

I decide to go with a frilly white summer dress with a ruffled skirt and puffed sleeves. It's casual enough to look like I didn't really mean to dress up, but it's also dressy enough so I'll blend in if he decides to go to a real restaurant.

I blow-dry my hair, put the finishing touches on my makeup, and slip into a pair of white ballet flats just before seven. I'm just putting on my jewelry when I hear the elevator ping outside.

My heart skips a beat when I head for the door to open it for Ellis.

I open it......and stop dead in my tracks when I see him. He's wearing a suit—a really nice suit.

I have to blink hard to convince myself that I'm really seeing this. He must be planning to go somewhere nice—like really nice.

He looks absolutely smoking hot in this suit. It perfectly accentuates his shoulders and the one button makes his waist look tight and muscular—because it is.

No one knows how muscular he really is because no one touched him in the elevator like I did.

I can't even remember the last time he dated anyone. In fact, he never has dated anyone in all the time I've known him. How did I not see how unbelievably hot he is?

His eyes widen when he sees me in my dress. His gaze roves down my ruffled top. He doesn't try to stop himself from appreciating my chest, my waist, and all the way down to my thighs.

"You look beautiful," he whispers.

His eyes make me weak in the knees. He wants me. He wants a lot of me, but he'll never take that step—not unless I tell and show him that I want him to.

I have to overcome this reserve that he has about me. I know he likes me and I know he wants to be gentle with me. That's the problem. I don't want him to be gentle.

Some inner beast lies sleeping inside him. I want to release it. I want to ride it. I want to feel all his power unleashing on me. I won't be able to build anything real with him until I do.

He joked about not being timid and subservient, but I still sense him holding himself back from me.

I don't wait. I dive through the door, grab his hand, and pull him inside.

I swing the door shut....and stop again. I want him here. I want him to do whatever he wants to me. I want him to take his reserve off its chain.

Once I get him inside my apartment, I don't seem to be able to do anything but stand here and look at him.

I want to take him and for him to take me all at the same time.

His eyes shine with so much meaning. He knows what I want....and he also sees that I can't do it by myself—I mean, I could, but I don't want to. I want him to want me enough to do it.

He doesn't move in and kiss me. He just stands there holding my hand.

His eyes dip ever so slightly to my dress again....and back up.....

I tremble in front of him in sudden fear. Did I go too far by bringing him in here?

I really don't know what he's capable of.....but I sure do want to find out. I don't want to wait anymore.

He doesn't move except to stand there and stare deep into my eyes. He can see me quivering all over with excitement and anticipation.

I want to touch him the way I did in the elevator. I want to tear that suit off him—and yet he looks so unbelievably mouth-watering in it.

He radiates charisma and confidence in that suit. He looks nothing like the wild young jokester from the firehouse.

I have a hard time remembering the wild young jokester from the firehouse when I look at this tall, built, stately man in front of me.

Very, very slowly—so slowly I can't possibly mistake what he's going to do—he slips his hand out of mine, eases close to me, and takes hold of the hem of my dress.

He lifts it slowly, deliberately......Every caress of the fabric against my skin makes me tingle. He knows why I pulled him into my apartment. Now he's doing it and there's no going back.

He pulls the dress over my head and my hair cascades over my neck and bare shoulders. I feel so exposed and raw like this. I feel so much more vulnerable to him than I did in the elevator.

He couldn't see me there. He barely touched me even when we did it.

It was all over in an instant. That won't happen here.

He lays the dress on the couch next to me.....and returns to the same place to look at me.

I stand before him in my bra and panties—completely unguarded. I'm at his mercy—and yet this feels so right.

Standing here for him to look at turns me on beyond my wildest fantasies. Not even doing it in the elevator turned me on this much.

I'm not sure doing it in the elevator turned me on at all. I can't remember why I did it except that I wanted him. I didn't want to wait for him to initiate it for me.

His eyes graze down my chest, around my breasts, and down my stomach to my panties. Can he see how wet he makes me just with his eyes?

My channel swells with hot juicy goodness. I throb in aching hunger for him, but he doesn't move.

His gaze devours me in such ravenous madness, but he controls himself to the limit.

He finally eases forward, and very slowly, drags the back of his knuckles over my skin. "Mmmmm," he breathes. "So beautiful...."

I gasp in a sudden moan of desperate agony as he trails his knuckles down the outside of my bra cup to my stomach.....and then takes his hand away.

I'm going to die if he doesn't touch me right now. I need him so bad!

He stands back like he really needs to think about whether he's going to go through with this. Can't he see that I'm his for the taking? How much more obvious can I make it?

He takes my hand, rubs my fingers once in a comforting gesture, and then turns away to lead me to my bedroom.

He's been in my apartment before. He knows where everything is.

He has never been in my apartment like this before.

He stops me by the bed and holds me in the sway of his all-consuming eyes while he unclips my bra and slides it off.

He lays it aside on the chair and then sits down on the bed. He turns me toward him and glides my panties down to my feet for me to step out of.

I rest my hand on his shoulder to balance myself and he lays my panties aside, too.

I see him going through all these little rituals. He decides where I go and what I do. He decides how fast we go and where we do it.

He barely looks at my slit or my breasts when he undresses me.

He stands up in front of me again and murmurs, "Lie down on the bed."

Chapter 16: Jessie

I sit down on my bed and then swivel my legs onto the bed. I lie down on my back in front of Ellis, completely naked. Now he can see me. I'm his. He knows that now.

I can't stop shaking with all this energy building inside me. Every inch of my skin prickles for his touch.

He sits down on the bed next to me and finally, finally lets his hungry gaze travel down my body.

My nipples harden under that unflinching gaze. My breasts heave as my breath shortens and rasps with every tortured inhalation.

My slippery nectar cools and fizzes on my swollen tissues. He must see how turned on I am.

Maybe seeing me like this excites him just as much. Maybe seeing me like this is what makes him slow down and enjoy how much he possesses me.

He doesn't touch me right away. He just sits there looking.

He looks so masterful and intoxicating in his suit. He really looks like a man who could own a girl just with a look.

I can't believe I'm falling so easily into his grasp, but isn't this what I wanted?

When he does touch me, he lays one hand on my opposite thigh, strokes it a few inches, grips, and then shifts to the other thigh.

He crawls one more painstaking inch toward my pulsating, saturated slit, but he doesn't go any further than that.

I pant and whimper for more. I can't help but raise my knees a little bit to try to rub my thighs against his hand, but my actions only make him hold back.

He moves his hand up to my arm, strokes it up and down, and then pets my hair.

His warm palm glides down to my face....and then he stands up before he bends over and kisses me.

He kisses me with his mouth open and his hot tongue dancing and slithering around mine. I try to put my arms around his neck to pull him in, but he takes them away and very gently lays them back down on the bed.

He doesn't outright tell me not to touch him, but his hands make it all too clear.

He only kisses me for a minute before he pulls away and starts kissing down my body. He kisses my collarbone, then the other side of my upper chest, and delivers a gentle, loving suck to each of my nipples.

His mouth skyrockets me into a torrent of excitement. I squeal as the first spikes of exhilarating passion hit me, but he's already moving on.

His saliva cools on my nipples and stimulates them to rock hard tingling madness. I writhe on the bed seething in pathetic moans.

I want him to touch me. I want him to take me, but he won't even lie down with me. He stands over me fully dressed—and he doesn't show any sign of getting undressed anytime soon.

He kisses down my stomach and takes a few deep succulent mouthfuls of my thighs. All this teasing gets me hotter and wetter than I ever thought possible.

I try again to raise and spread my thighs. I need something inside me even if it's just his fingers.

He eventually decides it's time for him to give me the first sensual lick to my aching petals. I sob in agony, but he only flickers his tongue between my dripping lips for an instant before he straightens up.

He looks down at me with a much different expression on his face. He no longer looks gentle or innocent.

His eyes blaze with a different kind of ferocity. His gaze snaps from one part of my body to another much quicker and with a much more commanding, almost critical fire. What does he see when he looks at me like that?

I stare up at him in blazing passion. I can't get enough of him. I want him so bad it drives me out of my mind, but I can't move off this bed when he looks at me like that.

He told me to lie down. I don't dare to move until he tells me to.

He keeps his tone just as soft, as low, and as breathless as before. "Turn over on your stomach."

I roll onto my stomach, but I stay near the edge of the bed so he can touch me if he wants to.

He sits down next to me again.

I start out stiff and hold my breath waiting to see what he's going to do.

He lays one hand on my back between my shoulder blades, slides up, and massages my neck and shoulders with big, warm, deep squeezes.

I melt in his grip, relax into the bed, and shut my eyes. His hands feel fantastic. They send waves of passionate warmth and desire through me. I can't hold myself stiff and tense when he touches me like this.

I let my head sink into the bedspread. He works one hand down to my shoulder blades, and before I think he might do something else, he slides his hand down my waist to my hips and finally my ass.

He crushes my ass in one hand, and in a split second, he seizes both my ass cheeks in his hands, twists, and pulls my ass cheeks apart.

"I dreamed of seeing you like this in the elevator," he husks. "I dreamed you would give yourself to me like this....that I would see you all glistening and ripe like this....."

He pries my ass cheeks apart just enough for the air to hit my damp tissues. The air cools them just enough to tell me loud and clear how wet I am for him.

Lightning quick, he plunges his face between my legs from behind. He pulls my ass cheeks apart so he can get his face and mouth all the way down between my thighs, but he holds my legs together so I can't spread them.

His hands pull me up and my own arching moans lift my hips into the air to get his full face into my juicy opening.

I moan and then scream as his scorching tongue touches my slit. He plunges in deep and I dissolve in a blistering orgasm on his face.

I try to push back against him to increase the pressure, but he won't let me. He keeps my ass up and tilted forward. He pushes my ass cheeks apart so forcefully that he actually holds me down on the bed.

This position excites me so much. I want so much more than this, but he's already giving me the most mind-blowing pleasure imaginable.

I get lost swimming in all this orgasmic bliss. I don't realize what's happening until he lets go, sits up, and goes back to where he was sitting on the edge of the bed.

I collapse still moaning and trembling with delight as wave upon wave of pleasure passes through me.

I clamp my eyes shut and concentrate on just being here in this cloud of rapture. I don't know what he's going to do to me next, but I couldn't function to go out to dinner now. I sure hope he doesn't ask.

He rubs my back a few more times and pets my hair. He doesn't touch me any other way....until without warning, he passes his finger ever so lightly up between my thighs.

His finger barely grazes my throbbing flesh. He's just excited me to an epic pitch of sensitivity and I yell out in an agony of sudden explosive sensation at that feather-light touch.

I'm still moaning and whimpering from that when he murmurs, "Turn over, precious girl."

I roll onto my back, but I can't look at him. I can't cope with how I feel about him after what he just did to me.

I want to crawl into his arms and hide there, but he doesn't give me a chance to.

I can't stop sobbing in brutal ecstasy when I lie down on my back. I turn my head away so I won't see him looking at me with all that powerful, hungry masculine fire of his. He isn't done with me. He hasn't even started.

He squeezes my thighs a few more times. That touch should comfort me, but it only reduces me to more pathetic moans. I need him more than anything—and he knows it. He knows he can tease me to endless pleasure and I'll always surrender to him.

He sees me trying to hide from him, cups my cheek, and turns my head so I have no choice but to look up at him.

I almost burst into tears when I see all the desire and heartfelt emotion brimming in his eyes. He loves me. His eyes would convince me even if he didn't say it.

That's why he holds off on taking my body and conquering me the way he knows he can. He loves me. He wants more—so much more.

I'm more than a beautiful body for him to play with—but I'm that, too.

Now I'm here for him to play with, but he still holds off.

He passes his thumb across my lips in such obvious passion. I don't have to see to know he's raging hard for me.

His smoldering eyes zero in on my lips. "What would you do with these lips if I let you?"

"Ellis....." I choke.

His eyes dart up to meet mine. "You are so incredibly beautiful, sweetheart," he whispers. "You're almost too beautiful to touch."

I gulp and grimace at the thought that he won't touch me.

He will, though. He already did and he'll do it again.

His eyes drag down my body to my breasts, and like a long-forgotten dream, his hands migrate to my breasts, too.

He pinches, teases, and excites my nipples until I cry out in ragged torment.....and then he slides down to my stomach.

He passes his flat hand across my stomach a few times....and drifts to my trembling mound.....

I start to try to spread my thighs again. I already know he doesn't want that, but incredibly, he drops his hand down and starts circling my clitoris in tiny, wicked rings.

I yell out as a thrilling wave of energy hits me. Impossibly fast, he grabs me by the back of the head with his other hand, grips his fingers in my hair, and crushes my mouth in a brutal kiss while he fingers me for the ages.

He rubs my clitoris faster.....and harder.....His circles get tighter and more insistent....

His tongue shoots into my mouth and I explode on his hand in another dizzy climax. His mouth muffles my screams as I crest the wave and crash into a torrent of mindless convulsive thrashing.

I try to buck against his hand, but he's already plunging his fingers deep into me. He tears his mouth away, crams his forehead against mine, and pants into my mouth as I scream and sob and bellow out all the catastrophic pleasure bursting from every part of my body.

I can't fight this and I don't want to. My hands fly to his shoulders, his arms, his hands—but I don't want to stop him. I just need to hold onto something solid in this storm.

I spasm again and again on his fingers. His eyes drill into me from inches away. He holds me tight against the torturous explosions splitting me in half. I want to beg him for this and so much more.

He holds me there so I can't move or get away. He wrings every drop of pleasure from my body that it can possibly give him before he lets me go.

Chapter 17: Jessie

Ellis eases his fingers out of my hair and his other hand out of my saturated channel. My tissues are so sensitive that every graze sends me spiraling out of my mind.

I can't keep lying here flat on my back. I'm too raw and fragile. I curl over on my side. I want to put my arms around him, but I can't reach him while he's still sitting there on the edge of the bed.

I slip my arms around his waist, shut my eyes against his jacket, and sob in the last throes of passionate bliss as the quivering tremors of pleasure torch through my body.

He hugs me once and rubs my back a few more times. I really can't stand it if he tells me to pull it together and get dressed to go out to eat.

He pets my hair once more and then I gasp out loud when he flips me back onto my stomach.

Before I know what hit me, he falls down on top of me, pins me under his weight, and wraps on arm around my upper chest from behind to hold me there while his fingers drill into me a second time—from behind this time.

I scream out, but he isn't taking any prisoners this time.

He crams his hot mouth against my ear and hisses out his molten breath through gritted teeth.

Every muscle swells to the breaking point as he holds me there and brings me to another crushing orgasm. I can't stand this....and then I feel him.

He draws his fingers out for a fraction of an instant and his thick, rock-hard shaft slips into their place.

I barely have time to gasp at the sheer power of what he's doing to me. This is nothing like what we did in the elevator. That was a teenage collision in the heat of the moment. It meant almost nothing, but this does.

Sweet Jesus, what was I thinking when I thought I wanted him to let his reserve off its chain? I got way more than I bargained for and he isn't about to let me come down.

He pumps into me from behind, holds me down on the bed, and husks in my ear with animal ferocity. His body tenses to a wall of granite behind me.

All thought that he might be some innocent boy too timid to take what he wants—it all goes out the window in a cosmic overflowing tumult of explosive climactic destruction.

I collapse under his weight and let myself buckle in the tremulous pulsations rippling around his shaft. He brings my juices bubbling from the depths to surround him and gush down his veins to welcome him in.

I don't know how long he keeps going. I don't know much of anything anymore.

I do know that I'm still peaking on the cresting streams of stratospheric space when he eases off and turns me over.

He rolls me onto my back and leaves me sprawled there whining and sobbing in blistering ecstasy while he takes his clothes off.

I fall with my thighs open and my arms above my head. I can only writhe here in front of him and let him see how inflamed and electrified I am by everything he's doing to me.

He rips off his jacket, yanks his tie loose, and flicks open his shirt buttons too fast.

He throws his clothes over to the chair where he left my bra.....and then all the muscles of his chest and shoulders bulge when he tugs his belt loose.

I get another scorching gut load of adrenaline when I see him taking his clothes off. His eyes narrow when he looks down at me. He doesn't take his eyes off of me once.

He rotates off the bed to stand next to it while he pushes his pants off. Then he climbs back on and moves back onto his knees between my spread thighs.

I moan in desperation watching him get into the position that he wants. I shiver when I see his tool sticking straight out at me ready to take me. It's going to claim me. It's going to conquer me. It already h as.

He watches me seethe in front of him trembling for him. He knows I'm his. He doesn't even have to ask.

He lifts me by the small part of my back to arch me into him. He surrounds his waist with my thighs and draws me in. He never bends over to accommodate me. I'm his to take his pleasure from.

I shriek again and spasm backward as he slides in. My body acts of its own accord and answers the rippling wave of his body moving into me.

He blasts me full of unstoppable energy every time he rises on his knees to thrust all the way to the hilt. I skyrocket into outer space on earth-shattering torrents of pleasure and power with each of those thrusts.

I can only fall back in his masterful grip and let him fill me with every inch of his iron length. The quivering sensation of explosive pleasure rushing down my channel and out to every corner of my body—it won't stop as long as he keeps taking me.

I start to lose awareness again of where I am and everything he's doing to me. Right then, he scoops his hands up under my back and lifts me off the bed.

He raises me to straddle his hips and I find myself riding him the way I did in the elevator—but this is nothing like that.

I can see him right in front of me. The lamplight shines in his soft eyes overflowing with love and majesty.

His arms cradle my body and guide me into his thrusts—and now he can see all the catastrophic emotion pouring out of me as he takes me to the stars.

My thighs surround him with his shaft buried deeper than deep in my throbbing channel. He keeps pumping into me with powerful, punishing strokes.

Each one of those thrusts drives me upward and knocks me senseless from below as he shatters my mind and body into breaking screams and epic explosions.

The look in his eyes won't be denied. Our encounter in the elevator wouldn't have been an innocent, teenage quickie if I could have seen him like this.

I would have drowned in him the way I'm drowning now. I would have gasped and panted out all my torturous longing into his mouth when he tries to kiss me. I would have sobbed and groaned in all the ecstasy he gives me through his powerful body.

I would have touched his cheeks and hair like this in such awe that he could give me this experience. I would have fallen into his thrall knowing he could take me as brutally as that and still love me this much.

His lips swirl in mine, but his eyes leave no room to hide. I don't want to hide anywhere but in his eyes.

I want to fall apart in one crushing orgasm after another and let him see that I'm his. I want him to feel how much my body belongs to him and how I ache to feel him buried inside me.

His lips and tongue hold me in a sea of rapture while his body takes me—and then his thick rod spasms once. He gasps out and his hot load floods me to overflowing.

This position makes it gush out over his shaft and down my ass and thighs. My body softens even more when I feel that. My hips slacken to sink deeper onto him. My puffy channel ripens thicker and juicier than ever to take him again and again.

He topples backward onto the bed with me still strapped around his hips. He lowers me onto my back, props himself above me, and keeps kissing me while he strokes into me one torturous inch at a time. Will he ever go soft?

His body clenches all over at the highest contraction of his thrusts. His eyes couldn't go any softer. They fill me with so much agonized longing for something I can't even define.

I can't get enough of just kissing him, gazing deep into the bottom of his soul, and feeling his body stroking into me. I've never experienced bliss like this. I never want to feel anything else ever again.

He drifts off my lips and pushes himself a little higher on his arms, but he doesn't stop stroking at the same rhythm.

He stares down at me with the same wide-eyed expression of awe and painful love.

He cocks his head once to study me closer. I struggle to control all the emotion coming to the surface right now. I love him so much it makes me almost cry.

"I love you," he whispers.

Those words hurt too much for me to answer. I try to speak, but no sound comes out. I can only make the shapes with my mouth, *Love you.*

Touching his face like this and feeling our bodies swaying togeth er.....this is everything I ever dreamed of. Nothing exists outside this moment, but it can't stay that way.

He suddenly bursts into a magical grin without breaking his rhythm. "This isn't what I had in mind when I invited you out to dinner."

I can't stop staring at him. I don't feel hungry at all even though neither of us ate anything in the elevator. We didn't even get a chance to eat on our shift afterward.

I haven't eaten a decent meal since I went to work yesterday morning, but I can't think straight enough to feel hungry.

So much pleasure floods my body. It consumes my every thought. It obliterates every other sense and awareness except this forgotten submerging in him.

He never stops his endless gliding in and out of my channel. My saturated tissues offer no resistance.

These luscious surges of power and pleasure don't stop. They gush to the edges of my being and dissolve every barrier separating me from him.

"You'll just keep taking it as long as I keep doing this, won't you?" he murmurs. "You'll never stop."

I can barely make a sound when I whisper, "Yes! Don't stop!"

He keeps going. His eyes take in every flicker of my expression and every ounce of heartfelt emotion passing between us.

"You're magnificent," he murmurs.

I can't even vocalize how magnificent he is. He's something so far distant from what I thought he was.

I never would have believed he could do what he just did in the last few minutes....or is it hours?

He decides on his own to pull out. It's a good thing that he does. I couldn't.

He's still hard as a rock and he can feel that I'm as receptive as ever.

He stays there on his hands and knees kissing me for a minute before he stops that, too. "We need to eat, sweetie. We're going out to dinner."

He pushes himself up on his knees and moves over to sit down on the edge of the bed.

I still feel tingly and sensitive from all the orgasms he's given me. My body doesn't know what to do with all this energy, now that he isn't inside me anymore.

I curl over on my side the way I did before. I feel fuzzy and brainless.

He sees me, picks me up, and sits me sideways on his lap again, but he doesn't start anything. He kisses me a few times and then steers my head down on his shoulder.

I shut my eyes and float into a dream world. I don't know or care about anything as long as I feel his arms around me.

I lose track of everything but his hands stroking me, petting my hair, and his lips coming to rest on the top of my head.

Chapter 18: Ellis

The perfume of sex coming from Jessie's skin and body makes me dizzy, but I have to sit here and be quiet while she comes down from the cosmos where she's drifting around in a daze.

I press my lips to her hair and shut my eyes as torrential memories consume me of what I just did to her.

She actually let me take her. She let me handle her and own her and conquer her like that. She actually climaxed when I did it to her like that.

She's unimaginably sweet and so, so intoxicating. I have a hard time keeping my hands off her—and now I know she wants it.

I know what I'm going to be thinking about all through dinner, but I have to wait for her to come back first.

She's trembling too badly to be asleep. I love how fragile and responsive she is. Her body belongs to me. I don't even have to ask.

I have to be careful how I touch her so I don't excite her again.

She curls up stark naked on my lap. I'm naked, too, but I don't feel any temptation to take her again—not now. I'll have all the time in the world to enjoy her delights as much as I want.

I can think of a thousand things I want to do with her and games I want to play with her. I'm going to have a lot of fun with her, but I have to take care of her right now.

I wait for the shivering to die down. She wilts onto my shoulder and buries her face in my neck still whimpering. Even kissing her is too much for her when she's like this.

I don't want to wait any longer and I don't think staying here is good for her, either. Don't ask me how I know this. Call it instinct.

I lay her down on her side on the bed, put my suit back on, check my hair in the bathroom mirror, and take her shoes and dress back to the bedroom.

She lies sprawled on her side with her hair scattered and her eyes closed. She looks wrecked. She looks truly conquered.

My nuts ache when I see her like this, but I want to see her sitting across from me at the dinner table, too.

I stroke her body once to get her attention and murmur in a low undertone, "Turn over, sweetheart."

She rolls onto her back and her hair spills over her face. I slip her delicate, slender feet into her panties and pull them up to her hips.

I love the way they close over her frilly pink petals. I want to kiss them again before we say goodbye, but that would lead to other things.

She lifts her hips for me to put her panties back on and then I take hold of her hands.

I pull her off the bed, stand her in front of me, and put her bra on for her. She stands there with her head down and her hair tumbled over her face while I handle her. She's mine. We both know it.

These beautiful breasts, this gorgeous stomach, this round, ripe ass I love so much—all mine.

She squirms into her bra and then raises her arms so I can pull the dress over her head. She raises her haunted eyes to meet my gaze when I tug the dress into place.

I let myself kiss her once then. "You're beautiful," I murmur. "You're a dream come true."

She doesn't answer. She complies with everything when I bend down to put her shoes on her feet. She's ready to go.

I take her hand, lead her to the living room, and she grabs her little white clutch from the hall table on our way out of the apartment.

She doesn't say a word on the way outside. She takes her place in the passenger seat and leans her head back to look out the window while I drive her into town.

By the time I park outside the restaurant and help her out, she looks and acts like any other girl. She doesn't act like I just conquered her a dozen different ways in her bedroom.

Her skin and eyes glow with sex. It blasts into me from inches away, but I'm the only one who notices it.

I lead her by the hand into the lobby. She huddles close to me while we wait for the maître d' to seat some other people before he comes for us.

He bows his head to me. "Table for two, Sir?" he asks.

"Yes, thank you," I tell him.

He shows us to a booth in the very back of a very busy, crowded restaurant glistening with crystal and silver. Opulent chandeliers sparkle overhead and water runs down a giant rock formation in the center of the restaurant.

Tropical plants and small trees grow around the water feature. They hide us from the rest of the diners.

We sit down in a dim corner with candlelight glowing on the table between us.

I pull out Jessie's chair for her and push it in before I sit down across from her. The maître d' disappears, comes back with a bottle of wine, and pours two glasses for us before he vanishes again.

Jessie glances around at everything. "Did you plan this?" she asks after the maître d' leaves us alone.

"I made reservations after we left the firehouse." I touch my wine glass to hers. "We're a little later than I expected, but it was worth it."

She glances around again and cringes lower in her seat. "I wish you would have told me we were coming somewhere as fancy as this. I feel extremely underdressed."

"You look fantastic," I tell her. "You look exactly like the woman I want on my arm when I come to a place like this."

Her eyes dart back to me. "Don't tell me you've come here before."

I can't help grinning and I feel my cheeks burning. "I haven't come here on a smoking hot date like this one if that's what you're asking. I've never had a date like this one—ever—with anyone—so you don't have to worry. You're the only one."

"*Have* you ever been here before?" she asks.

I can't stop blushing at her. She makes me so deliriously happy. "If you really want to know the truth, I came here with my parents. My great-aunt came to town for a very rare visit and my parents wanted to take her somewhere nice. That's the only time I came here—and I was only fourteen at the time. I was extremely uncomfortable and couldn't wait to leave."

Her eyes skate around the restaurant one more time. She actually looks terrified.

"Hey! Look at me," I tell her.

Her eyes dart back to me.

"Just concentrate on me. We're here together. You're here with me. None of the rest of this matters. You know me. I'm still the same person."

She doesn't answer. Her eyes change their expression ever so slightly.

She isn't terrified of me, but she doesn't think I'm the same person. Am I?

We just did it—and not the way we did it in the elevator.

Doing it with her like this changed me. I don't know how.

I couldn't have put on this suit and brought her here to this restaurant if it didn't change me. I don't know what I am, but I'm different.

"Drink your wine," I tell her.

She picks it up and takes a sip. Is she still in the trance she was in when we did it? I need to be careful with her if she is.

"Talk to me," I tell her. "Tell me how you're feeling."

"How I'm feeling about what?" She catches herself looking around at the waiters again. One of the nearby couples gets up to leave. "Do you mean fooling around with you or do you mean the whole elevator situation?"

"All of it. Let's start with the easy part. How do you feel about the whole elevator situation?"

She shrugs. "I don't feel anything about it except that I'm glad it's over. I mean....I'm not glad the part about us is over...."

I watch the interplay of expressions and impressions crossing her face.

I decide to change the subject. "When was the last time in the past year that you came over to my house?"

Her head shoots up. "What?"

"I can't remember what we did or if you came over. When was the last time you came over to my house?"

She blinks at me. "We didn't do anything. We never did anything before you got hit by that car."

"I know," I tell her. "I'm just curious."

"I think it was....." She runs her fingers through her hair and takes another sip of her wine. She's starting to loosen up. "Well, it was before John died, so I guess it would have been about seven or eight months ago."

I get distracted thinking about something else.

"Why do you ask about that?" she asks.

"I'm just thinking out loud. I should sell it."

Her eyes fall out of their sockets. "You would sell your house?! Why?"

"I would trade it up for something bigger—something with a backyard for kids—maybe something closer to the school. That's where all the other firehouse families live."

She gapes at me in horror. Now I know she's terrified.

"What?" I ask. "I told you I wanted this to be serious. I said I wanted it to be real."

She gulps and looks away. "You never said anything about that."

"What did you think I meant by serious?"

"I don't know! Not that!"

"Why not?" I take her hand off the table and squeeze it. "I want to marry you. I want us to be forever."

She flinches and looks away. She won't look at me at all now.

"Sweetie....look at me," I tell her. "I love you. I've never loved anyone the way I love you. I want this to be real. I want it all. I want us to raise a family and live happily ever after. Don't tell me you don't want it, too. I can't live without you."

She goes through another spasm of agony.

"Baby.....Jessie....." I murmur. "Look at me. Look at me right now. You're scaring me."

Her eyes snap over to mine. She has to stop herself from looking away again. "What?" she asks.

"Talk to me. Tell me you love me."

"How can you even say that?!" she blurts out. "How can you even be thinking or talking like that when you don't even know if you'll feel the same way tomorrow? How can *I* think or talk like that when *I* don't know if you'll feel the same way tomorrow?"

"I will feel the same way tomorrow." I hear my voice shaking. I can't let myself think about that—not when I have her sitting right here in front of me. "I love you. I'll always love you...."

"You don't know that! You don't even remember how you really feel about me."

"This is how I really feel about you, baby." My throat aches. I fight myself under control with an almighty effort. "I won't stop loving you when I get my memory back."

She pulls her hand out of mine way too fast. "You might not stop loving me, but you might stop wanting to be with me. You might stop wanting to talk to me or even look at me." Tears spring to her eyes, and out of my worst nightmares, they streak down her cheeks. "How can I bank anything on you with that hanging over my head?"

God, I want to hold her right now! I want to pet her and kiss her and make it all better.

She's crying right now because of me. I would do anything to make it better, but I can't.

I stretch my hand across the table. "Baby....just be here with me right now.....That's all I ask. Take my hand, Jessie....please."

She takes it, but she won't look at me.

Her hand feels velvety soft in mine. It reminds me of the rest of her silky, delectable body, but I can't think about any of that right now.

I'm just deciding how to break the awkward silence. This is definitely not what I had in mind when I asked her out to dinner.

Now she's sitting across from me crying her eyes out—because of me.

I would do absolutely anything to give her that assurance. Every particle of my being says that I'll always love her.

I can't remember it, but I would bet everything I own that I felt the same way about her in the last year.

I don't know what else was going on with me after John's death, but I do know my feelings for her didn't change. I didn't just wake up the morning after John's death and stop liking her.

I liked her for years. I loved her as a friend. I thought she was absolute dynamite and I still do.

Chapter 19: Ellis

J essie and I let go of each other's hands when the waiter comes to our table with our menus.

She bends studiously over hers and doesn't look at me while she reads it.

"I expect you to eat two days' worth of food—and drink a lot," I tell her over the top of my menu. "You could even order ribs. Just don't get sauce on your dress."

Her eyes shoot up and then, in answer to my fondest prayers, she grins and blushes. "You'll have to roll me into the apartment building."

"Then you'll be floundering on your giant stomach like a stranded tortoise and you won't be able to resist my advances."

She bursts out laughing and stifles it. She bends over her menu again and doesn't look up, but she keeps biting back grins and turning pink.

My stomach twists in knots watching her—or my own hunger may be getting the better of me.

"Screw it," I tell her and lay aside my menu. "I'm ordering the ribs."

She bursts into a full smirk and puts her menu down on top of mine. "Me, too. It will take me a week to get the stains out of my dress, but who cares, right? This dress won't even fit me after I'm done."

I find myself smirking back at her. "My diet and workout journal is going to hate me after this."

She grins more broadly. "Let's call this a one-time indulgence to make up for the last two days. After that, we'll get straight back on the treadmill."

Now I'm the one who grins. "Tell me you don't need to work out."

She pretends to gasp in horror. "Of course I do! What do you think—that I was born like this?"

I can't help but laugh, but we have to pay attention when the waiter comes. We order a truckload of side dishes of every imaginable kind plus a few different kinds of drinks.

She won't stop beaming at me across the table. "Just do me a favor, okay?"

"Name it. Anything you want."

She only gets slightly more serious, but she doesn't stop smiling. "Let's take forever off the table—for now. Only for now—until we know what's happening with you. We can have fun and enjoy each other and even love each other. I just don't want to start thinking like that until we know where we stand."

"But we don't know if I'll be like this from now on. The shrinks at the hospital said I might never get my memory back."

"Ellen told us the same thing—but it's only been a couple of weeks since the accident. Give it some time. I'm not going anywhere."

I'm not sure how to answer that. I want to start now.

I can start now. I can sell my house and buy a bigger one—one that will be perfect for kids. I can do all of that without ever saying the word, *forever,* to her again.

I won't tell her. She'll probably see me buy the house and move into it, but we can wait until she's ready.

We shoot the breeze and joke around until the waiter brings our food. Then it's all hands to battle stations for the hogs at the trough.

I take my jacket off and roll up my sleeves for this part. Jessie has an easier time because her sleeves are so short.

No one says anything for a long time, but we both keep groaning in an orgy of stuffing ourselves as we eat as much as we want.

"Don't ever let me get stuck in an elevator shaft again," she mumbles between bites.

I try to smirk at her, but it's a little hard with my cheeks bulging with food. "You won't be able to go off your diet if you don't get stuck in an elevator shaft once in a while."

"Nothing is worth that. I don't care what I eat as long as I don't go through that again."

I look up. "Was it really so bad—getting stuck down there with only me for company?"

She tries to grin and gets sauce all over her face. "You were the one thing that made it enjoyable. The rest of it I can do without—and I already have you out here, so I don't need to get stuck in an elevator shaft for that."

I suffer another somersault in my stomach. "You have me as much as you want. Everything we did down there, we can do up here."

She blushes again. "It's more comfortable out here, too."

"And the food is better."

She snorts on her barbecue sauce and starts coughing. I laugh at her while she tries to clean herself up and take a drink at the same time.

She finally cleans herself up enough to keep eating.

"You are such a bad date," I tell her. "I can't take you anywhere."

She laughs along with me. "Who do you think will give up first?"

"You, of course. You're half my size. Your stomach isn't big enough to hold all this."

She arches her eyebrow at me. "Is that supposed to be a challenge?"

I shrug that away. "I'm just saying. I can eat a lot."

She bends over her plate. "I don't feel like making it a challenge anyway. This is too much fun."

We go back to eating for a while. She doesn't even notice the other diners around us now.

They don't notice us, either. No one notices us rooting around in our food and grunting away like the pigs we are.

I find myself watching her across the table, but she only smirks at me. I love that she can go from serious about our future one minute and then letting all that go and enjoying herself the next.

She's everything I want. She's fun-loving and vivacious, but she's also serious enough to care for me with all her heart.

I don't have to ask if she wants forever with me. She wouldn't shed tears over it if it didn't mean a lot to her.

She never said she didn't want it with me. She just can't handle the uncertainty of not knowing.

That's okay. I understand.

I'll just have to give her as much certainty as I can—including sitting with the uncertainty and letting her sit with it.

One of two things will happen. Either I'll never get my memory back and she'll eventually realize we're always going to be like this.

The other possibility is that I will get my memory back. Then she'll see that I still care for her and I still want to be with her.

I don't envision any scenario where I don't want to be with her. I don't see how that would ever be possible.

She finally sits back in her chair, wipes her hands and face on her napkin, takes one more sip of wine, and drops the napkin in the middle of her plate. "I'm done. You win."

I chuckle at her. "Bow to the king, mere mortals."

She giggles and settles in to watch me finish. She won't stop grinning at me. "I think they might have a live cow out back. They can grill it for you if you really need to keep going."

I laugh and throw my own napkin down. "I'm done, too. I won't need to eat for another month."

She stretches her hand across the table to shake mine. "Congratulations. We'll find you a gold medal around here somewhere or other."

"Let's get out of here before someone calls the cops."

She laughs again, and this time, she takes my hand on our way out of the restaurant.

She smiles at me a lot more on the drive across town. We hold hands between the seats and I drive one-handed.

Her smile evaporates when I pull into the driveway of my house. It looks small, now that I'm thinking about having a family.

"What are we doing here?" she asks. "Aren't you going to take me home?"

I don't let go of her hand when I turn to face her in the seat. "Move in with me, baby," I murmur. "I don't want us to be apart anymore."

Her cheeks go white. "You said you wouldn't talk like that until we knew what was happening with you!"

"We aren't talking about forever. We're talking about right now. We're talking about being together every day and every night for as long as it lasts. If it doesn't work out, at least we'll have this time together." I squeeze her hand a little tighter. "Don't go back to your place. Stay with me here. I want you. I need you. I want all of you in every way." I lift her hand and kiss her knuckles just to seal the deal.

Her eyes dart toward the house. "I don't know....."

"Come inside," I breathe. "You don't have to do anything or decide anything. Just come inside. That's all I ask. I don't want to let you go so soon."

Chapter 20: Ellis

I get out, open the passenger door for Jessie to get out, take her hand, and lead her into my house.

My house isn't big. It's only three bedrooms, but it's bigger than her apartment. I switch on the light and lead her to the couch.

I keep a hold on her hand while we sit down next to each other. I should say something to break the ice.

"So how was your day at work today, honey?"

She smirks at me and snorts with laughter. "The plumber couldn't get the toilet unclogged. You'll have to do it."

I join in the joke. "How did your meeting go with little Johnny's teacher? Did he get in trouble again for sticking his finger up his nose in class?"

She explodes with laughter and nearly falls over. I take the opportunity to pull her against me. I lean back on the cushions and steer her in next to me.

She takes my cue, kicks off her shoes, and folds her legs under her while we cuddle together.

"Don't forget to pay that surcharge at the bank," she tells me.

I kiss the top of her head. "Thank you so much for the roast beef sandwiches in my lunchbox. They were delicious."

She heaves a long, shaky sigh. "Is this what it will be like?"

"No. It will be much better."

She sinks a little deeper into me. She doesn't answer for a minute. "You really want to do this, don't you?"

"Of course. I can't think of anyone I would rather do it with. What about you? Do you want to do it—apart from all the things you said that concern you about me?"

She sits up, but she doesn't pull away. She stays tucked into my arm and rests her hand on my chest while she looks into my eyes from right in front of me. "I do want to do it. I just....."

I lay my finger against her lips. "Don't say the rest. Just sit with it. Just sit with us both wanting it and call it enough."

I guide her head back down on my shoulder. I just want to sit here and feel her next to me. I don't want anything more.

She wants it and I want it. Who could ask for more than that?

I'm just settling in for a long comfortable evening. It's already been so perfect in every way. I would be happy to know that tonight was my last night on Earth.

Without warning, she raises her hand and rests it on my chest. The charge of energy radiates through my shirt and burns my skin. She wants more.

She slides her hand up my chest under my jacket—and I feel that electric thrill I felt in the elevator. She's touching me—like that. She's starting up again.

She strokes my chest under my jacket and then, out of the distance, she slides her hand between my legs.

Her touch sends a torch of fire straight to my crotch. She isn't even touching me yet, but I'm already getting painfully hard.

I cup her chin to look into her eyes. I see the depth of desire burning there. I have to kiss her.

Her mouth consumes me, and before I even know what I'm doing, she slides her hand the rest of the way to my package.

My shaft spasms in her hand when she squeezes. A thousand molten ideas rush into my brain.

My spunk is still running out of her slit right now. It's getting her panties wet and turning her on for me to take her all over again.

She rubs me stiff and still doesn't stop. I fight for air—and then her hand flies up to my belt.

I hardly dare to move when she tugs it open, unzips my fly, and burrows her hand into my shorts.

I gasp out in shock when her hand closes around my shaft. This is the first time she's touched me like this. I can barely survive the power rushing through me when she strokes my bare shaft to rigid hardness.

I can't kiss her even when she presses her lips right on my mouth. I can only stare into her haunted eyes from inches away. She's exciting me too fast for me to tolerate. I'm going to explode in her hand right now.

I try to thrust into her hand, but I can't do that very well when I'm sitting on the couch. She passes her hand up and down in a gentle gliding motion. The slowness drives me ballistic.

I sprawl backward on the couch feeling the ecstasy of her touch. I can't get enough of it. This is almost better than touching her myself.

In seconds, she breaks away from kissing me, dives into my lap, and takes me in her mouth.

I collapse back on the couch groaning and panting as the energy cycles higher. She holds me on the ragged edge of insanity with that hot, wicked little tongue of hers.

She coils it around me, swallows me all the way in, and eases back to tease me to the heights of ecstasy.

I don't know what to think. Should I unload into her mouth? Is that what she wants?

I can't move or speak to ask her. Part of me wants to grab her, shove my meat down her throat, and leave her breathless and sobbing.

I can't do that—not with her.

I don't get a chance even to think the matter through before she sits up and climbs on top of me.

This is a completely different view from the one in the elevator. Am I going to think about that every time she straddles me? I certainly hope so.

She smiles up at me in wicked pleasure when she settles her saturated panties along my length and rides me again and again without taking me inside.

Her wetness coats my veins. I could slip into her so easily. I could split her in half.

I'm enjoying it too much when she unbuttons my shirt, pulls off my tie, and then caresses her sweet hands all over me.

She lays my jacket and shirt open to expose my chest. Her hands electrify my skin.

I want her mouth on my chest and stomach, but she looks too beautiful sitting up like this.

Flashes of magnificent color wash over her cheeks every time she rides back on my shaft. Her nostrils flare and her lips pout in a delicious little shiver of delight.

Now it's my turn. I take hold of her dress, pull it over her head, and unclip her bra. I don't have the heart to tell her to stand up so I can take off her panties.

She's so wet that I don't have to. Her grinding motions move her panties aside just enough for her moist, swollen petals to surround me every time she arches her hips.

I sit back and watch her sway while I play with her hard little nipples. My pinches make her moan in delicious agony.

Her hair falls over her eyes in smoky, sultry passion when she closes her eyes. Then she yelps and throws back her head to arch her breasts into my hands.

I love watching her like this. I love the halo of sex shining all around her magnificent skin and hair.

I love it when she beats deeper. It only takes a slight tilt of my hips and I'm inside.

She throws back her head even more and screams out in wild abandon. Then nothing stops her from riding me until she drains every drop of me into her and buckles on my shoulder.

I stand up cradling her in my arms and carry her into my bedroom. She'll stay here. She just doesn't know it yet.

I lay her on the bed all rubbery and buzzing with sex. I pull down the covers and tuck her in all naked and blissful.

She whimpers just from the sheets dragging over her electric skin.

I leave the lamp on a little longer just so I can watch her float there in her sex-drugged haze.

I take my clothes off and skip the pajamas for tonight.

I slip in next to her, fold her in my arms, and switch off the light as we both sink into sleep.

Just for tonight, I can lose myself in the illusion that she's my wife. We have children asleep in the bedrooms down the hall.

We go back and forth between work, school, and all the kids' activities.

We sit on the couch and discuss our family business. We fall asleep in this bed every night and get up for work every morning.

This woman is my life. She's my joy and my heart.

I'll never let her go no matter what happens.

Chapter 21: Jessie

I drift awake out of a sound sleep—and freeze when I see Ellis right in front of me.

He lies on his side with his eyes open and stares at me from a few inches away. He must have been watching me sleep.

His eyes overflow with the same depth of feeling from last night—and from all our time together. He never stops looking at me like that now.

I shut my eyes again and pretend to go back to sleep so I can try unsuccessfully not to be aware that I'm lying in his bed.

He wants me to move in with him. He wants us to last forever and build a family together.

I can't handle thinking about any of that right now even though I want to do all of it. I want it so bad it scares me.

This is all going so fast. Why am I the only one here who is even marginally concerned about what will happen when he gets his memory back?

That on its own would be enough to scare me—and it does. It scares me a lot more than how much I want to spend the rest of my life with him.

He doesn't let me go back to sleep. He doesn't even let me pretend to go back to sleep.

He strokes his fingers through my hair. "I'm having dinner with my parents tonight. Come with me."

I let my eyes drift open. His expression radiates so much warmth and love. I would have to be blind not to see all the sexual passion mixed up with that love.

"You mean....you want me to meet your parents.....?" I ask.

He laughs at me. "You won't be meeting them because you already know them."

"But they would realize...about us....."

"You mean they would realize that we're a couple now?" He snorts. "That's the idea, sweetie. That's why you would come—so we could tell them."

I try to look away again, but his eyes won't let me.

"Is something wrong?" he asks. "Don't you want to see them so we can tell them we're a couple? I don't want to hide it from them. They've been telling me for years that I should get together with you."

"Are we a couple? Is that what this is?"

He laughs again. My God, he looks happy! He looks a thousand times happier than he ever did before John's death.

"We keep doing it with each other," he tells me. "And we love each other. I love you and I know you love me."

"Does that make us a couple?" I ask.

He blinks at me, but he doesn't stop being happy. He acts like just looking at me makes him indescribably happy. In fact, I know it does.

"What do you think makes us a couple?" he asks. "Or not a couple."

"I would think us deciding that we're going to be in a relationship would make us a couple. I would think we would have to decide that we actually were a couple before we actually became a couple. We can't decide any of that until we know what's going on with you."

"We did already decide that." He won't stop smirking at me like this is the most fun he has ever had in his life. "We decided that we would be together for each other as much as possible for as long as it lasts. We decided we would be together for each other until we find out what's going on with me, and when we do, that we would deal with it together. Isn't that what we decided?"

"When did we decide that?" I ask.

He compresses his lips and looks away, but he only does it to stop himself from smiling and maybe laughing again. "I can't remember when we decided, but even if we didn't, we could decide it right now. Isn't that what we're doing?"

I stare at him for what feels like a long time.

Don't ask me how, but it sure seems like we either already have made that decision or, curiously, that we're making the decision right now just by him saying it.

He comes back to gazing deeply, passionately, warmly into my eyes. "So what do you say? Do we agree that we're together based on that?"

"I guess so."

"Then will you come with me to have dinner with my parents? They adore you. They'll be thrilled that we're together."

"You never said anything about them trying to get you to go out with me."

He has to bite his lip this time to stop himself from grinning at me. "No, I didn't tell you."

"Why not?"

"Maybe because I never had any intention of asking you out before. I thought you were the greatest and I thought it was really sweet that they wanted us to get together, but I didn't plan to make it happen—not until after the accident."

I don't answer that one. It only brings up all the same questions neither of us can answer—like whether or not Ellis even wanted to have a relationship with me.

What if he never wanted it and the head injury did something to make him want it? What if whatever made him lose his memory also made him decide to go out with me?

He didn't just decide to go out with me. He decided to completely change our friendship which had been one of the longest-lasting relationships in both our lives.

What if whatever made him lose his memory suddenly reverses—and he suddenly remembers not just John's death but he also remembers why he didn't want to change our relationship?

He doesn't seem to want to ask himself those questions. He wants to forget all of that—just like he wants to forget how he felt about John's death.

He brings me back to reality by slipping his arm around me and pulling me closer to him in bed. "So will you come with me? It wouldn't look good if I went to dinner with them by myself and told them that you and I are a couple without you being there."

"I suppose I could."

He draws me in and kisses me. I kiss him back—and as soon as I do, the energy between us erupts back to life.

It lies just beneath the surface with the smallest hint of veneer keeping it hidden. It only takes a subtle kiss or suggestion to bring it raging into the open.

That kiss gets stronger, but he pulls away just as fast. He pulls his mouth away, but not his body.

He rocks his hips against mine to show me how hard he is. His body pulsates with powerful sexual energy.

He breathes heavily through his nostrils while he looks down into my eyes in smoldering passion. "You are so damn hot, baby," he breathes. "I can't get enough of you."

I gasp when his raging hard meat grazes the sensitive, swollen petals between my legs.

"Oooo, that's so good," he murmurs. "That is so hot and sweet."

I can't stop staring at him while he flexes his hips to stroke his wicked ridge up between the furrows of my molten slit.

His shaft excites all my blistering nerves lying exposed after last night.

He tilts his hips one last time and glides into me on a river of wetness. My body melts to open for him.

He shudders as a wave of intensity sweeps over him. His lips shiver and he sucks air through bared teeth in an animal snarl, but he doesn't take his eyes off me.

His hand flattens against the back of my hips and steers me into his slow, penetrating thrusts. My body lies open and receptive to his invading length.

My heart cracks at the same time. He invades everything that I am. I can't escape him. His body enthralls me and takes over my mind the same way he conquers my body.

I would probably lie here staring into his eyes and letting him invade me for the rest of the day. I can't think when he does it to me.

So much sensation and magical energy rushes through me when he slides his iron rod deep into my being.

Then he reduces me to a quivering mass of pleasure when he draws it out.

He eases off first. I don't come to my senses until he pulls out of me, kisses me for a few more minutes, and then retreats far enough for me to see the glowing look in his eyes again.

"Let's get up, sweetheart," he tells me. "We have to take you home to your apartment so you can get ready for work."

He sits up first. As soon as he gets out of bed, the moment dies and we both shift into autopilot mode.

I take a shower and put back on the dress I wore to the restaurant last night. He eyes me when I come out of the bedroom and I see him in his uniform.

He clicks his tongue in his mouth and shakes his head. "It's a good thing I won't be seeing you like that today. I might have to bend you over right there in the firehouse."

I blush and sit down at the table to eat the breakfast he made for me. "Let's not talk like that when we're both supposed to function today."

"It's a good thing we aren't working on the same truck today, too. I would have a hard time keeping my hands off you even in your uniform."

I bend over my food so he won't see me blushing, but he's right. We both need to pay attention to what we're doing today.

Chapter 22: Jessie

Ellis drives me to my apartment and goes inside with me while I change into my uniform and gather everything I need for work. Then he drives me to the firehouse in his pickup.

He parks behind the building and turns to me. "Are you ready for this?"

I blink up at him. "You aren't planning on telling everyone at the firehouse about us, are you?"

"Why not? We already went to one of the barbecues together. They already know about us."

I look away. "I'm not ready to go there with the whole crew—not yet."

"I don't see why not, but if it makes you more comfortable to do it this way, I can go along with it."

"Just don't say anything to them about it at all. Don't mention it or bring it up. If they already know, then you don't need to tell them."

"I don't understand why you have a problem with it."

I take his hand and squeeze. "If you're right and we wind up together, everyone on the crew is going to find out either way. You don't have to broadcast it to the four corners of the globe."

He laughs. "I don't have to, but I sure want to." He dives in and kisses me before he gets out of the truck.

He opens my door for me and hands me my duffel bag from the back of the truck.

No one seems to notice or care when we walk into the firehouse together. We go to the locker room together and then split up to work on our separate trucks.

By some kind of miracle, the subject of me and Ellis doesn't come up again for the rest of the day.

He works with Keith and Danny on the rescue truck, but I don't see him having a problem with them or vice versa.

I don't see as much of Ellis as I thought I would. That makes it easy to just focus on work. The subject of us as a couple or not a couple doesn't come up.

When I do see him and have to interact with him in the course of doing our jobs, he seems to be focusing on work, too.

That explains why neither Keith nor Danny has a problem with Ellis today. He doesn't constantly try to joke around and make the atmosphere lighter or more fun than it already is.

Maybe now he's getting the picture of why the atmosphere in the firehouse is so much more serious than it was before. Maybe now he's starting to understand why it has to be that way and none of us wants it to be any different.

I head for the locker room at the end of the shift and find Ellis already in there. We don't discuss it first before we leave together. No one mentions that, either.

He drives me to my apartment, but he stops me again when we park outside the building. "Get your things and move into my house," he tells me. "I don't want to keep driving you back and forth."

I stare at him and then look away.

He waits for me to say something—like maybe to tell him that I don't want to move in with him.

It would be so easy for me to go inside, take a shower, and change my clothes to get ready to go out to dinner with his parents.

Then he would go to his house and do the same thing before he picked me up to take me out.

We would probably wind up spending the night together at one place or the other and then we would have to go through this same discussion again tomorrow.

What's the point of doing any of that when we could just move in together?

I sigh and say, "All right." That's it. The decision has been made by someone somewhere along the line. I guess we're going to move in together.

He gets out from behind the wheel, opens my door for me, and follows me inside.

He sits on the couch and waits while I take a shower, change my clothes, and pack a bunch of other stuff into my duffel bag.

I bring my uniforms, casual clothes, bras and panties, and most of the other stuff I use on a daily basis. I feel like I'm going camping, but this is nothing like that.

I've lived in this apartment for five years. I should consider it a home, but I don't hesitate to walk out of it. I don't think I would even hesitate to walk out of it forever and never come back.

I will come back. I'll have to come back to move the rest of my stuff out.

I'm not ready to start thinking like that. I still have another three months left on my lease on this apartment.

I'll treat this whole moving-in-with-Ellis thing like I really am going camping. If it doesn't work out, I can just come back here. No harm, no foul.

He takes my loaded duffel bag from me and escorts me back to his truck. I make up my mind on our way back to his house.

I won't take it personally if he does get his memory back and decides to end it between us. I have to be prepared for that. I even expect it.

This is just a nice time. We'll enjoy it for as long as it lasts like he says.

I can't invest any hopes or dreams in what might happen afterward. I can't think about who or what he'll be when that happens.

I know and understand what he said about the doctors at the hospital. They said his memory might never come back. He could be like this forever.

I don't believe that for a second. Duke is right. A person doesn't just forget something as important as this.

One way or the other, Ellis will remember and then all of us will have to deal with the consequences.

For right now, I'm going on an extended camping trip to stay at Ellis's house. He carries my duffel bag inside and goes off to take a shower and change out of his uniform.

I sit down on the couch in the living room. I'm supposed to be moving in here, but I don't unpack my stuff. I'm not ready for that.

He comes out of the bedroom wearing clean jeans, a pair of tan work boots, and a dark blue button-up shirt over a white T-shirt. He leaves the outer blue shirt untucked.

I'm going for a casual look, too. I'm wearing a ruffle skirt and a cropped denim jacket over a white T-shirt with my white sneakers.

We look casual enough to meet Ellis's parents, but we still look good. He gives me a look before we leave for the restaurant.

We meet Ellis's parents in a much more casual family eatery downtown. It's loud and packed with families. Some of the kids scream in the background.

His parents make a fuss over me when Ellis shows up with me. "It's so good to see you again!" His mother kisses me on the cheek. "Look at you—all grown up!"

I have to laugh at her. "I'm no more grown up than I was at the hospital. How are you?" I hug Ellis's father. "It's great to see you."

We pass the usual pleasantries until we get settled at the table. Ellis and his parents talk back and forth about everything that has been going on since he got out of the hospital.

His parents ask me about work and everything, too. I always liked them and got along with them.

It means something different to know that they always wanted me and Ellis to end up together. Maybe his parents saw something in us that neither of us saw.

Ellis is talking to his father about a call we got two days ago. "I had to go to Chief Broebeck's office as soon as Jessie and I got to work this morning."

Arlen frowns at Ellis across the table. "What do you mean?"

"I mean I had to give him all the details on the incident. He has to file an incident report on situations like that."

"No, I mean the part where you said you and Jessie got to work this morning. You said, 'as soon as Jessie and I got to work this morning'."

Ellis doesn't miss a beat. "I drove her to work this morning—and I drove her home from work this afternoon. She moved in with me. We're a couple now."

Patricia gasps and both her hands fly to her mouth. "Really?! That's wonderful!" She pounces on me, squeezes my hand, and beams in my face. "I'm so glad! I always thought you were such a nice girl. I couldn't be happier."

I can't stop blushing. That went a lot easier than I thought.

I just mumble, "Thank you," and try to go back to my meal.

Arlen shakes hands with Ellis. "Congratulations, son! This is fantastic."

Ellis grins at his father and then glances at me. "I think it's pretty great myself."

That's it. That's the whole announcement taken care of. We all go back to eating and the subject turns.

Only once, Arlen asks Ellis, "So what are your plans together? What's next now that you're living together?"

"We aren't making any plans right now—not until we see what's happening with my memory loss. Jessie wants to see if I switch back to the way I was before or if the memory loss becomes permanent and I stay like this."

A cloud crosses his mother's face. "Oh. Of course. I didn't think of that."

"That's a good idea." Arlen points at me. "That's smart thinking, young lady."

"I'm sure it will be fine," Patricia interjects. "You were so sad before, sweetheart. It just didn't make sense that you could stay like that forever."

That's the end of the discussion. Ellis and his father go back to talking about the firehouse.

I find myself studying Ellis across the table. His features shine with more happiness than ever. He basks in the afterglow of his parents' approval.

They always loved him, supported him, and approved of him, but never as much as now.

They respect him too much as a firefighter and a man. Their respect, love, and admiration keep growing as he gets older, more mature, and more confident.

This decision to move in with me—or even to get together with me at all—it boosts him in their eyes even higher than he already was.

It boosts him in his own eyes, too. I've never seen him so confident and self-possessed. He's more than he ever was before.

Maybe this memory loss really is a good thing. Why would I want anything to deprive him of all this happiness? He and I wouldn't even be together if not for his memory loss.

Maybe I was wrong about this not being the real him. Maybe it will be better if he never gets his memory back.

He went silent and pushed everyone away because he couldn't let John's death go.

Maybe this memory loss is the trick he needs to finally be able to put it behind him and move on.

Chapter 23: Ellis

I come out of the locker room, take a look around the firehouse garage, and spot the usual people working on the rescue truck.

Jessie isn't working today, so at least I don't have to worry about that little distraction—that big distraction.

Keith sits in the front seat flipping the turn signal indicator off and on while Danny walks around the truck on the outside checking the lights.

He calls out to Keith when the light comes on and then they check the brakes and the overhead strobe bar.

"All good!" Danny calls.

Keith goes through the usual sequence of sending signals through the radio to contact dispatch for the start-of-shift radio check.

I climb into the middle seat to check my turnouts and my SCBA. Caleb is just finishing his. Carter and Sophie sit in the seat behind us going through the paramedics' equipment.

Caleb cranks his pressure valve open to check the pressure in his oxygen tank, turns it off, adjusts the hoses, and then puts his apparatus away under the seat.

I take mine out just as Sophie leaves to go do something. Caleb nods at the equipment in my hands. "Don't tighten the hoses past that line right there," he tells me. "See the two lines? Line them up together and don't move the connector past that point."

I frown at the mask and then at him. "Why not? It might not make a decent seal?"

"We already went through all of this with the maintenance crew. We were tightening the seals too much and damaging the O-rings." He makes a face and pushes open the door on his side. "You don't remember. It was your mask that had problems. Check the pressure in your mask. If it doesn't come up to pressure or if the connections leak, you need to turn in the mask and apparatus to Duke to get it checked out. Don't just tighten the connector and move on. That's the new protocol, so stick to it."

He climbs out of the truck and leaves me alone with my SCBA—except that I'm not alone. Carter sits in the seat behind me.

"The new protocol is that everyone on the crew is the new Fire Chief," I say more to myself than to him. "I'm the only firefighter left on the crew."

I glance over at him to see if he took the joke. He stares at me across the back of the seat.

His distorted features somehow make his eyes look even more intense than they normally do—or maybe it's just the way he's looking at me right now.

He only makes eye contact for an instant before he bends over the drug box. He finishes putting the ampules back into their places, latches the box, and slides it under the seat next to the jump kit.

Something in that look sets my nerves on end. I turn all the way around in the seat to confront him. "Do you have a problem with me?" I ask.

He looks up much more slowly. "I never had a problem with you, Ellis," he replies in his deep voice.

"Why are you acting weird around me, then? Everyone keeps treating me like an outsider. I'm trying not to joke around so much, but everyone keeps pushing me away."

"No one is pushing you away and I don't consider you an outsider."

He opens his door to get out, but I'm all done playing games with these people. A guy can only try so hard to fit in before he snaps.

I hustle after Carter on his way across the garage toward the training room. "Hey! I asked you a question! I'm doing my best to take the job seriously, but I can't help making the odd joke now and then. Everyone else on this crew is allowed to joke around, but not me. I might as well be wearing a bell around my neck to tell everyone to keep away from me."

Carter enters the training room and pulls open one of the supply cabinets without turning around. "No one has a problem with you joking around, Ellis," he replies over his shoulder.

"You could have fooled me." I rotate around him so I can get in his face from the side. "What is everyone's problem with me, anyway? What is *your* problem with me—and don't tell me you don't have one because I know you do! I'm not stupid. I can see you holding me at a distance. We're supposed to be friends—and I know the problem isn't me. I've never been happier—but that seems to be exactly what everyone's problem is. You all seem like you actually have a problem with me being happy."

"No one has a problem with you being happy," Carter replies out the side of his mouth. He won't look at me. "None of us could stand to see you so down. We would have done anything to help you out of that."

"Then why can't you be happy for me now? This memory loss is the best thing that has ever happened to me. It got me the woman of my dreams...."

I break off when I realize I may have said too much. I don't know how much Carter and the rest of the crew know about me and Jessie yet.

Even if they do know, they don't know how far it really has developed. They don't know Jessie and I are living together and working toward having a future together—or at least I am.

Carter's head snaps up, but he doesn't act like I said anything that surprises him. "You might be happier like this, Ellis. You're happier than you've ever been since John's death, but this isn't who you really are."

I smack my lips in annoyance. "Yes, it is! This is who I am. This is who I always have been for my entire life right up until John's death. I don't see why everyone wants me to be miserable by remembering the death of one of my greatest heroes."

His tone softens just a little bit, but the hard flinty determination in those deep, haunted eyes doesn't soften in the slightest. "No one wants you to be miserable, but this memory loss cost me the man who saved his life. Don't you understand that by now? That man who tackled Andy and saved my life is one of my greatest heroes and that man died when you lost your memory. You're more cheerful and energetic and outgoing now, but you lost something much bigger than your memory. You don't even know what you lost because you don't remember. You became something so much better after John died. You became more compassionate and caring. You gave everything to help your crew and the people who needed you. It brought you closer to all of us and made us respect you and admire you more. That's all gone now." He turns away shaking his head. "It's a damn shame because you were something truly exceptional—something none of us had seen in the service before. So you didn't talk. It didn't matter because we all loved you for it. We all trusted you. We all appreciated working with you on every shift. No one ever doubted you. No one ever had to wonder if your head was in the game because it was always in the game. That's gone now. I don't know if we can ever get it back."

He goes back to messing with the stuff in the cabinet. I can't even look to see what he's doing.

I stare at the side of his face in numb shock. This is it. This is the missing piece. This is what Jessie and Keith and the rest of them have been trying to tell me all this time.

I either didn't understand it or else....

Carter articulates it so much better than they do—probably because he's Carter. He understands these things in ways none of the rest of us do.

I changed. Jessie told me I changed, but I either didn't believe her or I didn't understand just how profound that change really was.

John's death changed me. It changed me into someone the crew likes and respects more than they ever did before. It brought me closer to them.

Now that man is dead. No wonder they've all been tiptoeing around me and refusing to look at me.

I can't imagine what I was like these last few months. Jessie talks about me like I was some kind of zombie. She even cries about it—and yet that's the person they all want to get back. They want some silent, distant, depressed husk of my former self instead of me.

I can't even decide to go back to that person they want me to be. Carter is right. I can't even remember what I was like, what I was thinking, or how or why I became what I did.

If I can't remember that, then I have no way to correct it. I'm trapped in this. I'm stuck as this outsider while everyone I care about grieves the loss of someone else.

Carter notices my silence and turns around to face me. His voice softens even more. He doesn't look or sound like a monster. He just looks and sounds like my friend—and I can't even remember that. That's the worst part. I can't even remember how we became friends.

He lays his hand on my shoulder and squeezes. "It would be better if you balanced the two instead of being one or the other. You're both. You can't be completely you without both. That's all any of us wants from you."

Chapter 24: Ellis

I pull into the driveway outside my house. Jessie's car sits in the driveway, so she's already home. Actually, she never left. She lives here now.

I have to sit in the driver's seat and think about it before I go in there. I have to decide how to face her.

Carter didn't tell me anything she hasn't been trying to tell me all along. He just said it differently—and it came across differently because it came from him.

I've never been anyone's hero before—certainly not their greatest hero.

I have a hard time accepting that I could be anyone's greatest hero the way John Brewer was a hero to me.

I find it even harder to accept that I could be that kind of hero to a man like Carter. He's so powerful, so confident, so self-possessed, and so ironclad determined in everything he does.

I already have a pretty good idea of why I tackled him the way I did. I admire him. I almost worship him.

I don't have the same relationship with him that I had with John. I spent a lot more years working for John. I barely know Carter at all.

I can't even remember our friendship. That part really kills me. He's such an amazing guy—and I saved his life.

He admires me for that. He grieves the loss of the man who saved his life—because I'm not that man.

I'm not even friends with him. I can't remember how or where or why or how he hired on with the fire crew. He's a stranger to me.

I share an even deeper bond with each of them. Keith. Danny. Billy. Caleb.

The same torturous heartbreak I feel over losing Carter—I feel it for all of them. Where the hell has my head been all this time that I could not see this?

And then there's Jessie. She's right here in my house—and yet she must have lost the person she cares for so much, too. I'm not that man. I'm not the man who was her friend.

I'm not the man she spent months trying to help out of a crippling depression. I'm not the man she shed tears over when her friend wouldn't even look at her.

That man is gone—dead. That man is just as dead as John Brewer.

I can only bring that man back by regaining my memory—and I can't even do that.

How can I even face her after everything I've done? How can I continue to have a relationship with her—the relationship I started—the relationship I insisted on and pushed so hard to build?

I can't spend the rest of my life in the truck. I have to face her no matter the outcome.

Maybe this is why I stopped talking to her—and to everyone else.

They don't say that's the reason. They say it brought me closer to them. Why didn't I listen?

I didn't let myself listen. I didn't let myself understand—not really. It took Carter to finally penetrate the fog of my own stupidity.

I get out of the truck and carry my duffle bag inside.

I walk in on Jessie working in the kitchen. She wears a long, loose, ruffly sundress and no shoes.

She looks succulent, domestic, and absolutely delicious like this—but I can't even go near her. I don't even want to think about how attractive she looks right now.

I have no right to lay a finger on her. I kick myself for even trying to do it with her. How crass and tactless that was —and now she's living in my house exactly the way I said I wanted her to.

I can't tell her to leave, though. I don't want her to leave. I want her here. I need her here.

She was the one who tried the hardest to help me before. We agreed we would get through all of this together. I have to at least try.

I sit across the kitchen counter and watch her work. She shoots me a blushing grin over her shoulder. "Hi, honey. How was your day at work?"

I can't take the joke. "It was about like you would expect. We had a callout for a kid at the elementary school who tried to take the cap off one of the storm drains and then stepped in it and got his foot stuck in it."

She laughs. "If only they could all be like that, right?"

I watch her in silence for a minute. She works with her back to me.

I should be able to admire how her dress gathers around her trim waist and then flares to surround her hips. I should be watering at the mouth when I see her ass moving under the flimsy fabric.

I should be getting hard when I think about her panties under her dress and her moist flesh waiting for me inside her panties.

None of those considerations touch me now. I know they're all there, but I can't even really get interested in them.

I almost get a sense that she belongs to another man. Her heart definitely belongs to another man.

That must be why she keeps pumping the brakes on us moving forward. She keeps waiting for her real man to come back and get her.

He's the one she thinks she's been doing it with all this time. He's the one she thinks has been touching her and kissing her all this time—not me.

She doesn't even know me. She doesn't even like me. She thinks I'm someone else.

She notices my silence and turns around to frown at me over her shoulder. "Are you okay? You're awfully quiet."

Quiet. I was quiet before. Now I'm talkative.

She should be happy that I'm getting quiet, but she isn't happy about it because I'm still not that man.

"I'm fine," I tell her. "I was just thinking."

"What's on your mind?"

I hesitate and then plunge in. I have to. I have to talk to her of all people. I can't keep her here under my roof without at least telling her.

"I had a conversation with Carter today. He....he actually explained to me why everyone is so uncomfortable around me—I mean, he explained it in a way that I could actually understand. I know you and Keith and Danny and everybody has already been telling me a million times, but I couldn't hear it before. I definitely heard it this time. I can't un-hear it."

She turns around to pour a steaming pot of pasta into the colander in the sink. "What did he say?"

I hesitate again. I cringe when I think about saying the words out loud.

"He said that the man I used to be—the man who saved his life—was one of his greatest heroes and that man died when I lost my memory. He says I became kinder, more compassionate, and more dedicated after John's death even though I didn't talk. It's true, isn't it? You said I changed, but you didn't say how. He said everyone loved me for it. He said they admired me and trusted me more like that—the way I used to be."

She stops what she's doing to stare at me over the counter. Her face registers no emotion at all. She doesn't even have to say, "Yes, it's true." I already know it's true.

I can't look at her. I can't hold her gaze. I feel like I should leave to get away from her, but this is my house.

I want to tell her that we can't be together. I'm not the person she thinks I am. I'm not the person she wants.

I don't really know what to do, but she reads my mind, comes around the counter to my side, and slips her hand into mine.

"You're still the same person," she tells me. "Don't you see? You still have all that care inside you. You just have to let it out. That's all you did. You didn't become more caring. You just didn't have all this fluff to hide it anymore. You gave yourself to your crewmates and the job. You helped everyone wherever they needed help. You weren't always putting on a performance to show everyone what a joker you were. None of that mattered. You could do the same thing now."

I barely glance at her. "I don't know.....Carter says I have to find a way to balance the two—and I don't even know how to. How can I when I don't remember what I was like before this?"

"He just told you—and I just told you. You were more caring, more considerate. You were more helpful to everyone and more selflessly dedicated to the job. You didn't try to perform for everyone and turn it into a circus."

I wince, but I can't even argue. That is exactly what I have been turning it into—a circus. I made light of the most serious, critical, dangerous disasters of my patients' lives. I turned their heartaches into a joke.

I hate myself for that, but I can't quit. The only alternative is to try to change.

Is this what happened to me when John died? Did I finally wake up and realize that the emergency services aren't just a giant playground for me to run around and play on?

These people I care so much about—they aren't interested in my jokes. They lost their brother, their father, their husband, their best friend, their mentor, their hero.

Every patient is that. Every emergency is that. That is the disaster I'm supposed to prevent every time I go out on a call.

Every patient I will ever meet is John Brewer. Every call is my one chance to save him and keep him alive for the people who depend on him.

Jessie goes back to the kitchen and keeps working. She sets the table for two and puts the food out for us to eat it.

This isn't a multi-course feast at a restaurant. It's something so much more important.

I asked for this. I asked her to come and live with me so we could build a life together.

Now she's making me dinner. We sit down on opposite sides of the table to eat.

I should talk to her. I should banter with her and engage her in conversation, but I can't think of anything to say.

Will it be like this when I go to work tomorrow? Maybe I'll never be able to say anything ever again, but I honestly don't even care about that.

Even keeping silent for the rest of my life would be better than making a mockery of the Fire service the way I have been. I can never let that happen again no matter what it costs—even if it costs me Jessie.

Chapter 25: Ellis

I pull into the firehouse parking lot, switch off the motor, and put my keys in the pocket of my uniform jacket.

I'm just about to get out when Jessie grabs my arm to stop me. "Hey! It will be all right. You're going to be fine."

I look down at her hand on my arm. It doesn't feel real. "I know," I mumble. "I'll be okay."

"I'll be right there if you need me for anything—and everyone here cares about you. You know that. Everyone here wants to help you."

I can only mumble, "I know."

Knowing they want to help me makes it so much worse. I can't believe I let them all down so badly. They're all so much better at this than I am.

They're all compassionate, caring, hardworking, dedicated professionals. Keith is right. I don't belong in the same building with them, but I have to be.

I lean in and kiss Jessie on the neck beneath her ear. I still have her.

"I'll be okay," I tell her. "Don't worry about me. Let's go. Let's get this done."

I get out, open her door for her, and take her duffel bag out of the back. We walk into the garage and the sea of noise swallows us.

We put our gear in our lockers and then head for our trucks the way we usually do. I put my head down and just get busy doing the job. I try to block out as much of the other stuff as possible.

I find my mind automatically switching over to trying to come up with jokes and snappy remarks to fill the airwaves.

I stop myself in time, but I realize as the morning wears on how obsessive this need has become for me.

Almost all my mental energy went into thinking up a constant stream of banter to make people laugh. I worked so hard and put so much effort and thought into turning every line of dialogue into a joke. What the hell is wrong with me?

I even feel myself having a desperation reaction that I'm not making people laugh. I'm not getting them started on funny lines of conversation that lead to epic punchlines.

Could this be some kind of addiction for me? I feel myself grasping at connections that aren't there. The connections aren't there because my constant jokes and banter stopped the connections from forming.

I don't let myself do it. I don't let myself make jokes or come up with funny quips. I just do the job and talk to everyone about the work—you know, the way I'm supposed to.

My mind goes into a tailspin trying to come up with a way to fill the void, but no one else notices a thing.

They all talk to me, give me instructions, call out suggestions and answers to questions, and go on with their jobs the same way. Nothing changes just because I stopped joking around.

The same flow of voices echoes through the garage even when I don't say anything. The world doesn't come to an end if I stop talking.

We get a call at ten o'clock. Josh and Carter are our paramedics.

"Car accident on the highway!" Billy reads on the computer. "Four cars involved! No word on the number of casualties! Police are en route!"

This would normally be the time when I would make a tactless remark about the call, but I don't say anything at all. What is there to say about a major motor vehicle accident? This is bound to be serious with possibly even a few fatalities.

No one notices that I don't comment on it. The crew must be used to me not saying anything. They don't think anything about me sitting here in silence.

Caleb, Danny, and I check our SCBAs. Josh and Carter talk about something going on with their drug box even though they just finished checking it less than an hour ago.

I don't have time to worry about that. I make sure all the seal connectors on my mask are set to the right position and then I check the pressure. I probably won't need to use the apparatus at a car accident scene, but anything is possible.

The apparatus is fine, so we concentrate on getting ready while Keith drives the rescue truck up the shoulder to the crash site.

We unload and get the initial report from Duke, but the scene looks pretty straightforward. All four cars lie crashed and overturned at odd angles to the flow of traffic.

Two of the cars lie upside down. Another lies on its side. The fourth rests on its wheels with most of its roof and passenger compartment smashed in.

The flattened roof doesn't look high enough for anyone to sit inside it—and it isn't. A single man sits behind the wheel with blood pouring down his face.

Duke divides us into teams. Caleb, Danny, and I get assigned to help Josh and Carter extricate this guy.

As soon as we get near the car, we see most of the side of his skull caved in just as badly. His left eye doesn't track right.

He starts babbling as soon as we get over there, but that side of his head isn't the right shape right, either. His shattered jaw garbles his words, but it's still impossible not to understand what he's saying.

"I'll kill him!!" he drawls and fades into partial unconsciousness before he rears back to life again. "I swear I'll fucking kill him!!"

Josh leans through the driver's window. "We're going to get you out, Sir! You need to go to the hospital! Can you tell me your name?"

"Where the hell is he?!" the patient raves. His one good eye tracks across the highway toward the fire trucks. "I swear I'll fucking kill him—the son of a bitch!"

"You'll kill who?" Josh yells over the noise and leans a little closer to shine his pen light into the patient's other eye.

"Get the hell off me, you son of a bitch!" The patient rounds on Josh and tries to lash out his fist.

Carter grabs Josh by the shirt and pulls him out of the window in time, but the patient never puts Josh in any danger. The guy can't see well enough to aim. He has to summon an almighty effort just to lift his arm.

"Stand back," Carter tells Josh. "You boys cut the patient out. Maybe by the time you get him clear enough to extricate, he'll lose consciousness enough not to give us any trouble."

The two paramedics back off while Caleb, Danny, and I lay out the Jaws of Life and cut into the car. We cut off the driver's door.

The patient keeps bellowing obscenities at everyone the whole time and threatening to kill someone. Two Police officers stand by to watch, but we can all see that Carter is right.

The guy keeps losing steam the longer this goes on. He strikes out at anyone who comes near him, including us, but he lacks the strength to hurt anyone.

His speech becomes increasingly slurred and incoherent, but he doesn't stop ranting about wanting to kill someone.

We finally tear off the driver's door. Caleb has no problem opening the rear passenger door, sliding into the seat, and trying to immobilize the patient's head from behind.

Josh leans in a second time and starts cutting off the patient's seatbelt. "We're getting you out of here, Sir!" Josh tells him. "Just hold on a little longer and we'll get you into the ambulance."

"Where is the son of a bitch?!" the guy roars. "I swear I'll kill him. Get your fucking hands off me, you bastard! I'll kill you! I'll kill you all!"

The guy thrashes so badly that Caleb can't hold him. Josh finishes pulling the shreds of the seatbelt away while I position a backboard on the driver's seat to pull the patient onto it.

He starts to slump and Carter moves in. He and Josh grab the patient, swivel him out of the car, and lie him down on the backboard. They don't wait around to try to immobilize his neck. He's too combative.

Caleb gets out of the back, now that the paramedics don't need him. The other teams are all using the ambulance gurneys to load up other patients.

Josh and Carter lay the backboard on the ground while they go over the guy as fast as they can to assess him, check his vitals, and hook him up to the defibrillator. It's only a matter of time before the guy codes on us.

I take a step forward with the restraint straps. We would have to strap the patient to the backboard for transport even if he wasn't combative and yelling abuse at everyone.

The crash caved in his skull. It must have damaged his spine, too. It's a miracle the guy is even still awake.

Carter moves down to the patient's arm, takes hold of the patient's wrist, and turns his arm over so Carter can start looking for a vein.

I have my hands full of the straps, but right at that moment, the patient erupts back to full alert, bellows one more time, "Get your hands off me, you son of a bitch!" and pulls a gun from his jacket pocket. None of us realized it was there.

Time slows to a standstill when I see the gun moving toward Carter's head. I drop the straps in a heartbeat and dive for the guy's arm to knock the gun away.

I don't want to move into the path of the gun myself, so I aim for the guy's forearm and tackle it to the ground.

The gun goes off right in my ear, a bomb goes off in my brain, and all my memories from the past year come rushing back.

Chapter 26: Jessie

Keith, Duke, and I stand in silence in the elevator on our way upstairs from the hospital lobby.

Ellis has been in the neurocognition lab for the last ten hours undergoing every test known to humankind, but at least he's still alive.

I have to stop myself from knitting my fingers together. I've been doing that so much that my hands hurt.

It took me hours to figure out exactly what happened to Ellis.

The fire crew had to spend the rest of our shift treating and transporting patients from the multi-car accident on the highway.

I didn't get a chance to talk to anyone from the rescue truck until it was all over.

"The gun went off right next to his head," Josh finally tells me. "He fell down screaming and holding onto his head. None of us could get a word out of him for the rest of the call. We threw him in the ambulance with the patient, and when we got to the hospital, I registered Ellis as a patient, too. That's the last time I saw him."

"Was he at least conscious when you left him?"

Josh squirms and looks away. "That depends on how you define, 'conscious'. He was completely out of his mind. He kept thrashing around and fighting everyone off. He was yelling the whole time, but he wasn't saying any coherent words that I could pick up. He was just going off. He was still like that when we left. The medical team restrained him and took him inside. I'm sorry. I can't tell you anything else."

"But you don't know if he actually got hurt, do you?" I ask. "You don't know if he actually got shot."

"He didn't get shot—but I can't say whether he got hurt or not. He had no visible external injuries—but he could have gotten some kind of traumatic brain injury that we don't know about. We didn't have time to assess him. We had our hands full with the other patient. It was pretty obvious that Ellis was at least physically stable even if he was completely out of control. We couldn't do anything—and then we got to the hospital and the ED staff took him. Ellen can probably tell you more when you get there."

That conversation doesn't give me any peace of mind at all. I would almost rather if Josh didn't tell me anything.

Carter stands off to one side listening to everything Josh says. So that confirms it. Carter must have seen exactly the same thing.

I fidget in the elevator. I dread what I'll find when I get upstairs and see Ellis again.

I've been so worried all this time about him getting his memory back. What if he completely loses his mind?

What if he never comes back—as any of the former versions of himself? What if he's completely gone mentally while his body is still here? What will I do then?

I don't think I can handle that.

This idea of me and Ellis staying together and building a life to-gether—it's starting to take over my whole idea of who I am. I don't want to let it go. I can't let it go.

I nearly have a heart attack when the elevator doors open in the neurocognition lab. The first thing we see is Ellen Foreman standing at the desk talking to the charge nurse and two other doctors in lab coats.

Ellen leaves the desk and comes forward to meet us. "I'm really sorry, but you're too late. Ellis already left. He checked himself out of the hospital." She waves at the doctors. "I just got their report right before you got here."

"What do you mean—he left the hospital?" Duke asks. "Josh said he was raving out of his mind."

"He was. He was raving out of his mind in ED, but that was ten hours ago. He calmed down pretty quickly, and after that, the doctors couldn't find anything cognitively wrong with him. He was obeying commands, following instructions, and he filled out all the paperwork perfectly before he left. He just wouldn't talk to anyone."

My hand flies to my head. "Oh, no! Not again."

She gives me the saddest smile. "I'm sorry, sweetie. The hospital had no legal basis to hold him. He's a competent adult. He had every right to sign himself out. He passed every test, including hearing tests on the ear closest to the gun when it went off. He had no injuries to his head, his eardrum, or any other part of his body—nor did he pose any risk to himself or others."

Duke lets out a heavy sigh. "I can't believe it. He saved Carter's life again and now we're back to all of that."

"I'm afraid so. Ellis never said a single word to anyone—not here, not in ED, not ever."

"Then how did he tell the doctors and nurses that he wanted to leave?" Keith asks.

She smiles again, but just as sadly. "He wrote it on a piece of paper. He wrote it out in perfectly neat, intelligible handwriting and used very exact, specific legal terminology to demand that the hospital release him. He even threatened legal action if they didn't expedite the process."

"Wow," Duke murmurs. "He must have really wanted to get out of here."

"Did he show any other sign that he was upset?" I ask.

"Not after he initially calmed down. He was completely off his rocker when Josh and Carter dropped him off. Five minutes later, Ellis was absolutely cold, deadly calm. He never blinked after that. He went through every test like a Terminator and passed them all with flying colors."

"So where is he?" Keith asked. "He must have left on foot. His truck is still at the firehouse as far as we know."

Ellen shrugs. "Your guess is as good as mine. Just remember that he's a mentally competent adult with full legal rights to make his own decisions. You can't go out there treating him like some escaped mental patient or even a dementia patient who wandered off. If he wants to be alone, you have to leave him alone. You can't make him do anything he doesn't want to do. He can make his own decisions. He has to make his own decisions."

I really don't want to hear that. I want the crew to bring Ellis back right now.

Duke, Keith, and I leave the hospital and drive back to the firehouse just as the shift is about to change again. Both of the off-duty crews meet us there.

"We'll split up," Duke decides. "We can cover more territory that way. Ellis's pickup isn't in the firehouse parking lot anymore, so he must have come back here and driven the truck somewhere. If anyone finds him, don't approach him. Just call or text the rest of the crew to tell us his location and if he's all right."

Everyone divides up into separate vehicles. We all drive off in different directions.

I go back to Ellis's house first, but I already know he won't be there. He wanted to get away from everyone. He would have contacted someone from the crew by now if he didn't want to be alone.

I check my old apartment next even though I already know he won't be there, either.

My blood runs cold when I unlock the door and walk into the living room. This place gives me the creeps now.

All my old thoughts about camping out at Ellis's house and coming back here if it didn't work out between us—all those thoughts go out the window in a heartbeat.

I don't want to camp out—and I will never, ever move back to this apartment.

Ellis is all right. He can function perfectly well mentally.

He won't talk to anyone. The gunshot probably brought his memory back.

I can reason with him. I can talk to him. I have to talk to him even if it means the end of our relationship. I have to hear it from him.

I get back in my car and drive around town for three hours. I check all the usual spots and even a bunch of unusual ones. I stop by every restaurant he and I have ever visited and I search the fun park from one end to the other.

I pass a bunch of the fire crew who are also out searching Howe with a fine-toothed comb. We don't stop to talk to each other. Someone would have contacted me by now if they found Ellis.

I start to panic when the sun starts to go down. Duke calls everyone to confirm that no one has found Ellis yet.

The crew changes at the firehouse and the old shift takes over, but we still don't find him. Duke doesn't ask me to go back on shift even though I'm rostered on.

I stop my car outside the fun park for the second time, but I don't go in there. I can't. I can't face searching for Ellis anymore when he isn't here.

He isn't anywhere in Howe, so he must have left town. He could be halfway across the country by now, but something tells me he isn't.

All his stuff is still in the drawers at his house. Nothing has been touched, not even his electronics.

He has to be somewhere.

Chapter 27: Jessie

I drive out into the country and eventually end up at the forest parking lot leading to the mountain overlook west of Howe.

Ellis has never mentioned coming here and his truck isn't in the parking lot, but it seems the most logical place for someone to come if he wanted to be alone where no one would find him.

I don't even know if he doesn't want anyone to find him. Something else may be going on with him.

I get out of my car. The sun is already sinking behind the horizon and the stars are coming out. It will be full dark soon, but I can't stop now.

I take a flashlight out of my glove compartment and set off up the path. I'm not dressed for this, but I have to do this no matter what.

I hike for an hour before I get to the overlook. I don't have to shine my flashlight over there to see Ellis.

He sits alone on the top peak looking out over the glimmering lights of Howe spread out below him. The dim light outlines his hunched figure sitting cross-legged on the rocky ground. He's still wearing his uniform.

My heart spasms for him. He remembers. He wouldn't come up here if he didn't remember.

I don't know what will happen to us or if we can ever be together again, but that doesn't matter. Nothing matters but him.

He's the man of my heart, the man of my dreams. I care about him beyond words. I want everything to be all right for him even if I can't be with him.

I switch off the flashlight, cross the peak, and sit down next to him. I want more than anything for him to look at me the way he did before—the way he's been looking at me with so much love and care these last few days.

I have to remember what I told him last night. He's still the same person. He's all those people combined into one.

He's the fun-loving boy who was my friend. He's the silent, dedicated firefighter who always jumps in to help anyone who needs it.

He's still the man who loves me. I know that now. He always loved me, even when he pushed me away. He pushed me away *because* he loves me.

He still loves me now even though he won't even look at me.

I slide my hand into his lap and take his. He doesn't respond, but he doesn't stop me, either.

He keeps staring out at the view. He doesn't say a word. So it's all true. We're back to that.

"Do you want to tell me what happened?" I ask.

He doesn't move except to blink at the skyline in the distance. His hands feel just as warm and strong as ever. Does he even know I'm here?

I feel myself starting to get choked up. If he doesn't talk to me, it's over. I just have to face that.

"I love you...." I croak. "Please.....just look at me...or talk to me.... .give me something."

Did he move just now....or did I just imagine it?

He doesn't look at me nor does he speak.

I gulp down tears, but they well up in my eyes anyway. "Is it over between us? I was right, wasn't I? You remember John's death and now you don't want to be with me anymore."

The anguish I've been keeping bottled up comes boiling to the surface. Tears streak down my cheeks. Now I have no choice but to walk away from him.

I'm more alone now than I was before we got together. I'm more alone now than I was after John's death.

I had Ellis then. I had a friend....and now I have nothing.

I see the bleak, lonely road in front of me. I'll drive back into town, go back to his house, gather up all my stuff that I just left there, and take it back to my apartment.

I really was just camping out at his place—counting down the hours until he got his memory back.

Now the whole fairy tale comes crashing down. It never was more than that. It was a distant dream with no substance at all.

"If you don't talk to me now, I'll assume you don't want to be with me and I'll walk away." I have to stop to stifle sobs, but he must be able to hear anyway.

A million other ideas come together in my mind. He's pushing me away because he loves me.

I hate him for doing this to me, but the pain overpowers everything else. I'm losing him. I already have lost him. He's already gone.

He said so many times that he never meant to hurt me, but he did mean to. He knew he was hurting me by pushing me away. He still did it knowing how much he meant to me.

He's doing it right now. He's deliberately destroying everything we had.

He won't overcome that simple hurdle just to talk to me—just a few words—for my sake—just to make me feel better.

How can he claim to love me if he does this to me?

I sniff back tears, but I'm too angry even to break down sobbing in front of him. I won't give him the satisfaction.

I'll wait until I get home to my apartment. Then I'll completely fall apart. I'll pour out all the anguish and heartbreak over losing what could have been the greatest love of my life.

I pull my hand out of his and push myself up. I barely manage to choke out, "Goodbye, Ellis," and turn away.

I cover my mouth to hold back my sobs at least until I get out of earshot. I don't want him to hear me. He already knows how much this hurts.

I make it halfway across the overlook before he calls out, "Jessie! Wait!"

I spin around fast. "What do you want from me?!" I shriek and all my anguish unfolds beyond my control to stop it. "How can you do this to me?! How can you hurt me like this when you said you wouldn't?! You broke my heart, Ellis! I never asked for any of this! *You* did this! You made me love you and now you won't even look at me!"

I break down sobbing my eyes out. I turn my back to him, but I'm crying too hard to find my way down the mountain.

I cover my face with my hands and unload all my misery right there. I don't even care if he hears. This has nothing to do with him anymore. He's already lost to me. What difference does it make when he doesn't even care how much I'm hurting?

Out of nowhere, his arms fold around me. His presence makes me sob even harder. I break down on his chest wailing my heart out.

He's the one who did this. He can't be the one who comforts me, too.

My grief and pain turn back into rage. I shove him away with all my strength. "Leave me alone!" I roar. "Don't you dare touch me after what you're doing!"

I turn my back on him again, but I still don't have the heart to leave.

"Please....don't leave...." he murmurs. "I'm trying...."

"Well, try harder!" I bellow. "Don't I mean anything to you at all?"

"Of course," he murmurs. "You know you do."

"How can I believe that?! You didn't even call me from the hospital! The whole crew is out there looking for you! How could you let me worry about you like that? How could you make me think even for a second that you didn't want me?!"

He doesn't reply. He just stands there in silence.

I hate him for that, but my own words hurt too much even for me to hate him. Those words are true. He cares more about himself than he does about me. He wouldn't leave me like this if he cared.

I finally throw back my head. I don't know how much of me he can see and I don't care.

"If you won't at least talk to me, then we're finished. We can't go on like this. You have to give me something. I can't just stand here loving you and get nothing in return."

He takes a long time to answer. Something in his silence tells me he really is trying. Maybe it just takes him an eternity to figure out what to say. Maybe that's the problem.

He finally takes a step closer to me in the dark. "Sit down......please......"

I don't want to listen. I don't want to soften. I don't want to give him another chance. I just want to get as far away from this pain as possible.

He doesn't wait for me to do it. He takes the last step toward me, slips his hand into mine with the same warmth as before, leads me back to the overlook, sits down in the same spot, and pulls me down on the ground next to him.

Sitting here makes me just as angry. Why am I even here?

His eyes rotate out to the horizon. He goes back into his trance.

"I don't know what to say," he mumbles under his breath.

"Say you love me and you want to marry me." I hear myself snapping at him, but all this raw emotion won't settle down so fast.

He turns his head even farther away. He murmurs under his breath in a dull undertone with no life or feeling at all. "I love you and I want to marry you. I just don't know how to."

"Just tell me what's going on!" My voice cracks—with anguish, this time. "Please....just tell me what's going on with you. Help me understand—for me. You don't have to do it for yourself. Just....please....do it for me."

"I'm trying," he murmurs. "I'm really trying."

"What do you see when you look out there?" I demand. "Why is whatever is out there more important to you than I am that you won't even look at me? You have to give me something to hold onto. You can't just vanish out of my life into this silence. This silence is the easy road. Don't you understand that? It's cowardly and selfish. I didn't ask for this relationship. You said we would work together to get through whatever happened. You have to do that now. You have to work with me. I can't do it alone. The whole relationship will fall apart if you do n't."

"I don't know how to love you," he mumbles. "I don't know how to talk about it. I don't know how to do anything. That's the problem."

"You aren't responsible for John's death," I tell him. "You saved Carter's life—and you saved him a second time yesterday. Everyone at the firehouse admires you. You have to know that."

"I know I'm not responsible for John's death," he murmurs. "I never thought I was."

"Then what exactly is the problem?"

"I just keep seeing it......" Now his voice is the one to break with buried emotion. "I keep seeing him.....lying there......on the sand.....with his head half blown off.....I can't stop seeing it.....It's always there.....right in front of my eyes. I can't even think. Even thinking or acting on the crew takes all my strength and attention. I have nothing left for anything else."

I stare at the side of his face and the puzzle pieces click again.

John....dead.....on the sand.....

That image flashes before my eyes....his head half blown off......

Of course. It all makes sense now.

"It keeps happening....over and over again in front of my eyes...." he husks. "It never stops....all this time when I couldn't remember.....that was the only time it stopped. I don't know how to do any of this......"

I can't listen to this. I understand now. I almost wish I didn't.

What a nightmare Ellis must have been living all this time. No wonder he pushed everyone away.

He pushed me away because he saw that he was hurting me. He couldn't help me by changing himself. He couldn't even help himself.

I dive for him. I don't even let him finish before I cup his cheek, turn his face toward me, and kiss him with all my might.

I would throw my arms around him and tackle him to the ground right now, but I don't even know if he wants that.

I cradle his face in both hands and just get lost in kissing him. I know now. I know because he told me. He does care. He cares enough to make us work—but I already knew that.

I ease back just enough to see his eyes in the light coming from Howe.

"I love you," I tell him. "The whole crew loves you. You can do this. You can do this exactly the same way you did it before. You called 911 to help those kids and the truck driver. You talked to Duke and Chief Walker. You talked to me in the paper plant. You can do this. You can get through this. I'll help you. You aren't alone."

His eyes dart down to my mouth and then back up to meet mine. His eyes swim with so much buried uncertainty and tortured anguish.

He just wants to be there for all of us. He wants to be the same man we all love and admire. He doesn't even realize that he already is that man.

I kiss him again—once. "Come on. Let's go home."

Chapter 28: Jessie

I take Ellis's hand and pull him to his feet. He follows me when I switch on my flashlight and lead him down the mountain to the parking lot.

I stop there and look around. My car is the only vehicle here. "Where's your truck?"

He jerks his thumb over his shoulder, but he still takes a few extra seconds before he can bring himself to actually vocalize an answer. "Over on the east side."

I have to think about it before I realize what he means. There's another trail on the other side of this mountain leading to the same overlook. He must have parked in the other parking lot over there and climbed up the east side of the mountain.

"Oh, okay," I tell him. "Get in and I'll drive you over there."

I switch off my flashlight and pull out my keys, but before I can walk away, he grabs my elbow and stops me.

He pulls me closer to him so I can see his eyes shining in the faint starlight.

He gazes deep into my eyes.....and I see the man I've been getting close to these past few days. This is the man I love. He's the same person.

His eyes radiate a combination of love, questioning, and a different kind of power. I've only ever seen that power from him in the deepest throes of passion.

Now he's the one who cradles my cheeks in both hands. He gazes at me for what seems like a long time.

That look in his eyes erases all the doubt and pain from my mind. I don't need him to talk. I just need him to look at me like this. I just need to feel this way when he looks at me and know that he still loves me as much as ever if not more.

He kisses me, but it's much slower and gentler than he used to. It isn't hesitating. It's just softer and he lingers there as if he wants to savor his last kiss on Earth.

As soon as his lips trail off my mouth, he draws me into his arms, but this is just the deep, warm hug of our hearts together at last. This moment crushes my soul in ways his kiss never could.

I hold onto him with all my might. I love him more than anything. I want nothing but to be with him. I don't even need to kiss him as long as I know he's all right.

He hugs me back just as hard. He buries his face in my neck and shoulder and he doesn't let go. Now I know he wants me. He needs me. He loves me.

He was telling the truth. His feelings for me didn't change—not at all.

We break apart and I smile at him. His eyes soften, but he has trouble smiling. That's okay. I can get used to the way he's acting.

I turn back to the car and get a sudden brainwave. I open the passenger door, make eye contact with him, and give an elaborate sweeping bow to wave him into the seat. "Your chariot, Kind Sir."

He snorts with laughter once and his cheeks flush as he gets into the seat. I laugh, too—mostly in relief. Everything is going to be all right now.

I get behind the wheel and stick my keys into the ignition. "Just hold on a sec," I tell him. "I just need to text the crew to tell them that I found you."

He sits in silence while I send out a text to everyone on the crew to say that I found Ellis, that he's all right, and that I'm taking him home. I tell everyone that I'll contact them later if we need anything.

They all text back to say that's great and they all go home.

I look up to find Ellis studying me from the side. He watches the light from the phone shining on my face.

"You okay?" I ask.

He nods.

I can't help smiling when I squeeze his hand. Then I start the car and drive him around the mountain to the other parking lot. I park next to his truck.

"I'll see you back at home," I tell him.

He kisses me one more time and gets out.

I drive off into the night, drive back to his house, and switch on the lights. This house means something different now than it did just this morning. I never want to lose Ellis.

The life I had with him before didn't seem real. A part of me never fully believed that he was real or that any of what he said and promised was real.

Now I know it is. He doesn't have to say it out loud. I know how he feels about me. I know what kind of life he wants to have with me.

I don't have to doubt anything about him anymore. He is very, very real. Everything he does and says is as real as I could hope it would be.

He remembers the last year. He remembers all of it, even the parts he would rather not remember.

His silence brings us closer together exactly the way Carter said. It only makes me love Ellis more.....and it somehow makes it easier for him to show that he loves me.

His truck pulls into the driveway and the door slams. He approaches the front door and enters the house slowly. He doesn't move around with the same energy. He has a hard time looking at me when he sees me there.

I go over to him and squeeze his hand again. "It's getting late and you're rostered on shift tomorrow. Let's go to bed. We can deal with reality tomorrow after we both get some sleep. Come on."

I go into the bedroom and start changing out of my uniform. It's already eleven-thirty at night.

I put my uniform in the laundry and get out the long T-shirt I wear as pajamas. I go into the bathroom to brush my teeth and hear Ellis in the bedroom taking off his boots.

I bend over to spit out the toothpaste and rinse my toothbrush. Then I put it away and turn off the light to leave the bathroom.

Before I can turn around, Ellis comes up to me in the dark, wraps his arms around me from behind, and crushes my body against his.

His hot mouth comes to rest on my neck and then leaves a scorching path of fire up to my ear as his hands take hold of me.

He grinds my ass against his hard package while one hand slides up to my breasts under my T-shirt.

His other hand dives between my legs and finds the cleft of my panties.

He starts on the outside with my T-shirt. It separates him from my bare flesh, but that doesn't last long before he plunges his fingers all the way inside my panties.

I gasp as spiking desire and blistering heat take over. He seizes me with every ounce of his old ferocity. Why did I think he suddenly forgot that he feels this way about me?

I'm in his house, in his bedroom, about to get into his bed with him. What else would we be doing?

The darkness melts the distinctions between all the different shades of Ellis I've been seeing these last few days.

There are no different shades of Ellis. He's just one man.

This power always waited inside him for the right circumstances to release it.

His fingers swirl in my tissues and bring the slippery nectar dripping from deep inside me. He circles my clitoris in rapid, expert strokes that make me whine in desperation.

His other hand clamps on my soft breast through my T-shirt. His ravenous mouth keeps mauling my neck, ear, shoulder, and even around my neck to my back.

His primal madness takes hold of me and ignites my deepest desires. I want him. I want the man who has been taking me to the stars these last few days. I want him to conquer me and possess me as only he can.

He pushes me forward to bend me over the bathroom counter, plunges his fingers into me to make me scream....and eases off.

I don't understand the problem until he straightens up and turns me around to face him.

He moves in on me to kiss me. His eyes glisten with so much hidden passion, but the same dark question hangs over both of us.

I don't understand that question. I want him more than ever. I want to throw myself at him and have him tear me in half, but he doesn't.

He pulls me in and kisses me for the ages. His lips and hands flood me with warmth.

He doesn't try to hide how hard he is, so why doesn't he take me?

Chapter 29: Jessie

Ellis leaves the bathroom first and we both go back to the bedroom without discussing it first.

I crawl under the covers while he changes out of his uniform. He puts on his thin plaid flannel pajama pants, gets into bed next to me shirtless, and switches off the light.

We both snuggle together and he puts his arms around me. Maybe he didn't want to do it after all. Maybe he just wanted to let me know he still could—that his desire still burned for me—but he doesn't want to do it right this minute.

I can't say I blame him after the day he just had.

I'm just starting to relax back into the bed to let myself drift away when he pushes himself up.

He rolls me onto my back, props himself on his elbow, and kisses me again. Just enough light comes through the curtains to show me his haunted dark eyes. He keeps them open while we kiss....and then he rotates on top of me.

He lies on top of me with all his weight and works his body between my legs, but he doesn't go any further than that.

He stays there above me kissing me endlessly. His eyes keep drilling me with that same question.

I spread my legs for him to push in against me, but he does every-thing slowly.... impossibly slowly..... and so agonizingly deliberately.

He never rushes anything. He studies me with every move. What is it he wants to see in me or find out from me?

I find out soon enough when he starts to get hard again. His kisses build to a slow burn. His tongue invades my mouth a little deeper. His heat blazes hotter.

It starts in a volcanic surge out of the mists of time. He starts so slowly that I don't notice it at first, but it's always there burning just below the surface.

I feel him get hard first....and then he flexes in to grind against my panties. His hand slides up the back of my neck to steer me tighter into his mouth.

Everything he does takes control of how fast we go and what we do—and he never breaks eye contact even once.

All those questions—all that power—it smolders in his eyes beyond time, beyond anything I can imagine. He's here. He wasn't before, but he is now.

He remembers everything we did to get us to this point, but he also remembers everything else. He remembers all the months when he pushed me away and held me at a distance.

He still wanted me this much even then. He has to overcome his resistance to take me like this.

He eases off just enough to push up on his knees and lift my T-shirt over my head. He peels it off and sinks back on top of me. Now I'm only wearing my panties.

He wraps his arms around me and lies down on top of me exactly the same way he did before. Will he ever do anything else?

He kisses me endlessly....until the moment when he doesn't any-more. He breaks away, dives down to my chest, and inhales my nipples into his mouth.

His sucks spiral me into my mind. I thrash underneath him as his mouth teases me to my limit.

I try to grind on him and he drills into me harder. He doesn't hold himself back this time. He corkscrews his hips to arch his throbbing package into my panties.

I whimper and moan as he teases me. I want him to touch me all over.

I can't stop clawing at his bare back and shoulders, but he only holds me tighter. Did I really think anything would change or that he somehow forgot that we could be like this?

Without warning, he raises his head, locks his mysterious eyes on me with unbreakable power, and pulls his pajama pants down just enough to slip past my panties to my waiting channel.

I stare up into his eyes in the breaking realization that he's taking me. He's inside and stroking beyond gently.

He doesn't kiss me. I'm too enthralled by his power to even try to kiss him back.

His body flows in a never-ending wave of muscle to pulse his hot shaft into my sensitive flesh. My wetness surrounds him and my inner walls clamp around him.

My lips shiver and I fight for air as his shaft excites every nerve ending all the way in and all the way out.

He clamps me in his chiseled arms. I can't get away. His meat pumps me so full of energy that I feel myself about to explode.

He stays there, inches above my face, consuming every trace of my expression with dark, commanding eyes. He sees me losing my mind in the cosmic desire for his power.

I tremble on the crest of a huge climax, but his eyes hold me there in his thrall. He searches and studies every shade of my being while he watches me crumble into his grasp.

Every thrust asks the question. My moans answer. I'm his for the taking. I can't resist him. I want him to possess me in every way he wants to.

He does possess me. He possesses me beyond all reason. Every thrust claims me. Every moan answers that I'm his. I whimper in front of him in pathetic agony for release, but his eyes don't let me go.

I feel myself starting to fall apart in desperate need, but right then, he pushes himself up on his arms. He glares down at me in all his majesty.

That one movement gives me the space to spread my legs wide for his thrusts. I raise my arms to hold onto his neck. Now he can see my whole body undulating and surging with the waves translating through his muscles.

That one shift in position sets me off. I try to turn my head away and shut my eyes against the sheer magnitude of the torrent breaking out of me, but I can never escape the hypnotic power of his gaze.

I stare up at him and let him see me spasming, twitching, and sobbing in front of him as all my desire pours out around his shaft. I succumb to the catastrophic blasts of light and heat bursting my body and soul into the stratosphere.

He hovers over me watching and listening to my screams. My channel convulses around him in searing heat until he pumps in extra hard and ejects his hot load as deep inside me as he wants to.

That feeling of his essence drizzling from my slit propels me into another reeling climax. I thrash and struggle underneath him. I scream out in all my aching hunger for him, but I already have him. He's right here with me and giving me exactly what I most need.

He sinks down on top of me and brings me back to my senses by kissing me. He eases off, shifts to the side, and rolls onto the bed, but he doesn't pull out.

He leaves me to power down at my own pace until I slip off him and scoot down to huddle in his arms.

I'm still sobbing and whimpering in the last ebbs of bliss. I shut my eyes and lower my head, but I only wind up resting my forehead against his temple.

I become distantly aware of his heart hammering through his sternum and his strained breathing sinking back to its normal rate. I was too far out of my mind to notice how much this affected him.

I huddle against him. His muscular torso shelters my sensitive skin from the storm still raging inside me. He still turns me on beyond anything I've ever known.

I want him again. I want him a thousand times, but we're both already drifting.

His warm, protective arms close around me and pull me into his heat. He tugs the covers over both of us. His soft, gentle hands stroke my electric skin, but he does it firmly so I don't get too turned on. We both need to go to sleep now.

His voice drifts out of the darkness into my ears. "Do you still want me if I'm going to be like this?"

"Of course!" I whisper into his ear. "I always want you no matter what you are. I still love you. I love you more than anything."

He turns his head just enough to kiss my forehead. "Marry me," he whispers. "Don't ever leave me."

I attack him, but this position doesn't give me many options for holding him. "Yes!" I whisper back. "I will."

His arms clamp around me tighter and he lets out a shuddering sigh of breath and sinks into sleep.

His breathing lengthens. His body relaxes and his hold on me slackens, but only when the rest of him completely lets go.

I stay awake watching, feeling, and listening to his breathing. He's so beautiful and precious to me.

He's more beautiful and precious to me like this than he was before. Everything Carter, Duke, and Keith said about him is true.

We can all love him so much more easily now. He's so much more accessible. We can all see his beautiful heart laid out right there on his sleeve—exactly where it should be.

God, I love him for that! I love that he remembers John's death and how much it devastated all of us, including Ellis. I love that he's back to being one of the crew now. I never have to worry about that ever again.

I already know what will happen tomorrow when he goes to work. Everyone at the firehouse will be thrilled and relieved that he's finally back to the way he was—back to the way he's supposed to be.

I finally let my eyes sink shut in the softness of his embrace. I can let myself sleep now knowing that everything is all right.

Chapter 30: Ellis

I take a deep breath before I get out of my truck and go into the firehouse. Facing the crew will be hard after everything that happened last night, but I have to do this.

I just have to remember what Carter, Keith, and Jessie said. The crew wants me like this. They want me the way I was before. They all love me. They love me even more because I'm quiet.

Part of me doesn't want to believe that even though I know it's true.

I have to do this for Jessie, but I have to do it for myself first. This crew is where I belong. I don't want to wait another minute to find out where I stand with everyone.

I already know where I stand. I just have to get over the hurdle of walking in there, facing them, and then we can all go back to work the way we're supposed to.

I take my duffel bag out of the truck, grab the lunchbox Jessie made for me, and stash it in the side pocket of my duffel.

She made me breakfast this morning and packed me lunch. She slept in my bed last night. She called my house, *home*. I can't stop thinking about those words. *Let's go home.*

We're living together and she said she wants to marry me. I want that so bad. Part of me doesn't want to believe that, either, but I want it too bad to back out on it.

My heart flips just thinking about her. I have her. I can face anything as long as I have her.

I only have to think about her living in my house and smirking at me across the breakfast table. Those little flashes of mischief in her eyes and the blushes on her cheeks give me superhuman strength to face any challenge, no matter what it is.

I walk into the garage the way I do for every shift. The crew is already there working on the trucks. Keith, Billy, Caleb, Josh, and Carter all stop what they're doing when they see me.

Keith scowls at me and arches his eyebrows. "You okay, buddy?"

I nod down at the floor.

His heavy, powerful hand clamps on my shoulder. "We're all glad to have you back. We all missed you."

My throat hurts. I wish like anything I could look at them, but their care and affection means too much.

I love all these guys more than I can stand. I just wish I could show them.

Keith gives me a shake. "Come on. Let's get after it. You can help Billy check the truck lights."

"Shit, you scared the crap out of us when we thought you got shot," Josh tells me.

"Can we not allow anyone to bring any more firearms to calls?" Caleb asks. "We're going to have to make the Police search all our patients if this keeps up."

"That dude was out of his flippin' mind," Billy counters. "You know his brain got half squashed in the wreck."

"That wasn't the reason at all," Carter chimes in. "The guy is being charged for road rage. He was the one who caused that wreck. He was waving the gun around in the middle of traffic and trying to shoot at other cars. He got caught in the same wreck. He's already being charged even when he's still in ICU."

"Are you freaking serious?!" Billy fires back. "I didn't know that."

"Jim Walker told me. That's why the patient had the gun in his pocket. That's why he was raving the whole time about wanting to kill someone. He wasn't altered at all. He was like that before the wreck ever happened."

"No way!" Caleb whispers. "I don't believe it."

I stare across the circle at Carter. The story surprises me so much that I don't think to look away until he makes eye contact with me.

There's no challenge in his eyes. He includes me in his circle of listeners. I'm just part of the crew.

"Are we done solving the world's problems?" Keith interrupts. "We have a job to do here."

We break up and go to the trucks. Billy climbs into the cab. I stand at the front and wave to him when he turns on the turn signals, the overhead strobe bar, and then I walk behind the truck to check the brake lights, reversing lights, and the rear turn signals.

I'm just giving him the thumbs up in the rearview mirrors when Duke comes downstairs. He frowns at a few sheets of paper in his hands, scans the garage, and sees me standing there.

"Hey! Great you're back! I was gonna ask you if you want to pick up a few overtime shifts next week. Theo is taking some of his accumulated sick days so he can go on vacation. What do you say to covering his shifts?"

I nod.

He swivels over to stand next to me and points at the upcoming roster. "So I have you on the morning ladder truck Tuesday, Thursday, and Saturday. Then you're on the rescue truck overnight on Monday and Friday. Wednesday and Sunday, you would be on the ambulance covering for George—one shift with Chris and one with Sophie. You all good with that?"

I nod again and he claps me on the back. "Thanks, man. I really appreciate it."

He walks away and we all go on as before. Nothing ever changes around here.

We go into the training room at eleven-thirty. We're training on the nebulizers today.

For some reason known only to himself, Duke gets the idea that we should all test the nebulizers on ourselves.

"Only if you brought some really good drugs for us to dose ourselves with," Caleb teases.

Duke smiles at him. "Save that for your off-time, champ. I wasn't planning for you to use any drugs at all. Just use the nebulizer so you know what it feels like. Then you'll be able to coach your patients when you want to treat them for something."

He divides us into groups of four to a machine. I get paired with Caleb, Chris, and Danny.

Caleb turns on the machine and brings the mouthpiece perilously close to my face. "Open wide and tell me who killed Professor Plum in the library."

The other two laugh. "Professor Plum is one of the suspects, you moron," Chris tells him.

"Ellis is the only suspect here," Caleb replies, turns back to me, and waves the mouthpiece in my face. "Did you use the candlestick or the lead pipe?"

"I think we better do the first treatment on you," Danny cuts in. "That's the only way we'll be able to shut you up."

"No way," Caleb counters. "I'm the rescuer here. Someone else can be the patient."

"Help me restrain him, Chris," Danny tells her. "Ellis, you can administer the torture."

Danny and Chris pretend to grab Caleb by the arms and sit him down hard in a chair. "Hey!" he protests. "Get your hands off me!"

"Bring the muzzle, Ellis!" Danny yells over his shoulder. "Quick—before he gets away!"

I pick up the nebulizer, but right then, Duke comes over to us. "Quit screwing around. We're supposed to be trained professionals here."

"Speak for yourself," Danny counters and gets another laugh from both Chris and Caleb.

I'm still standing there holding the nebulizer. I'm not a part of this whole performance, but Duke's presence calms everyone down and we get back to practicing with the nebulizer the way we're supposed to.

I used to be the one who would joke around and make light of the training like that. Not anymore.

I'm not the class clown anymore, but no one notices that I'm not constantly filling the airwaves. No one seems to notice me at all except as any other ordinary member of this crew.

This feels good. It feels better than good. It feels great.

Everyone is so much more comfortable with me like this....and so am I. This is the way I'm supposed to be. I know that now.

Chapter 31: Jessie

E llis and I step into the same family eatery and meet Ellis's parents waiting there for us. I hug both his parents and then they both turn to hug him, too.

His mother's face drains of all color when she sees him standing there. I'm not sure what tipped her off—except that she's his mother. Of course she must be able to tell everything about him.

He barely makes eye contact with them and he doesn't come right out and talk to them the way he did before. His reserve couldn't be more obvious.

She blinks at him in horror. Arlen doesn't move for a second. The silence becomes deafening and Ellis doesn't say a word to break it.

That leaves me to explain things. "Ellis had an incident at work the other day. One of his patients pulled a gun on the paramedics. Ellis tackled the gun out of the way in time and it went off right next to his ear. He got his memory back—so he's back to being the way he was before the car accident—but don't worry. He's fine. He didn't get hurt in any way. He went back to work today and everything is going fine ."

His parents don't respond—not to me. Patricia gapes at her son. He won't look at them at all now. They can see perfectly well that he's back to his old quiet ways.

"No!" Patricia chokes. "No! It can't be!" She shakes her head and then starts sobbing, but she won't stop staring at him. "NO! You can't! You were so happy before! This is awful! Can't the doctors do something?"

I move in when I see Ellis starting to turn away.

I take her arm and make her face me. "He's fine. He isn't sad or depressed. He's working and Duke is as pleased as ever with Ellis's job performance. Everything is going to be okay." I pull her into the restaurant. "Let's go get a table. We can talk about this."

"But you....you can't seriously be thinking of.....you can't....you can't *continue* with this!" she blurts out.

"Continue with what?"

"You....and Ellis...." She turns around, takes one look at him, and starts sobbing again.

"Yes, we are," I tell her. "We're happier than ever....and we're getting married. Ellis proposed to me last night."

She stares at me out of huge, swimming eyes. "He what?"

"He asked me to marry him. He isn't in a coma. He's fine. He's great. You have nothing to worry about."

She looks at him and then she really does break down. She buries her face in her hands and bawls loudly enough to distract the other patrons from their meals.

I pull her the rest of the way to a table in the back, park her in her chair, sit down next to her, and Ellis sits down next to me with his father on his other side.

Arlen keeps casting terrified glances back and forth between me and Ellis. "Are you sure about this?" Arlen murmurs to me out the side of his mouth. "I mean....he's so distant."

"No, he isn't. He's just quiet." I smile across the table at Ellis. He makes eye contact with me just enough for me to see how agonizing this conversation must be for him.

I turn back to Patricia and squeeze her arm. "Everything is going to work out. You'll see. Ellis wants to sell his house and buy something bigger—something with a backyard and closer to the school so we can start a family. Hey! Come on! I need your help to plan the wedding and everything. This is nothing to cry about!"

It takes her a long, long time to pull herself together.

"Are you sure?" Arlen asks again. "Aren't you worried that.....?"

I turn to face him. "Worried that what?"

"That...." He casts a sidelong glance at his son, but Arlen won't really look at Ellis, either. "Aren't you worried that he'll change back? He's been changing so many times lately."

"Not really—I mean, I'm not worried about it—and he hasn't been changing so many times. He changed the first time after John Brewer's death—which was a pretty traumatic blow for all of us. That's when Ellis stopped talking. Then he got in the car accident that affected his memory. This latest gunshot just brought his memory back. Don't worry about it. The doctors at the neurocognition lab at the hospital ran every test they have a name for on Ellis. They couldn't find anything wrong with him."

"Not physically," Arlen murmurs.

"The psychiatrists ran every test they have a name for on him after the car accident," I point out. "They didn't find anything wrong with him psychologically then, either. He lost his memory. They predicted that the loss would be temporary and they were right. Now Ellis has his memory back. He remembers John's death and what made Ellis stop talking in the first place. As far as I'm concerned, this is the way he's supposed to be."

Patricia glances at Ellis and dissolves in another attack of bitter tears. "I just want my son back! Why can't I have my son back?!"

I stand up to go over there and hug her. I kneel down next to her chair so I can talk to her at her own level. "You have your son back. He's right here—and he's wonderful like this. I love him and I know you do, too. Be happy for us. Be happy for me. He's the kindest, bravest, most caring man I know and I can't wait to marry him and start a family with him. Just think of that. You two are going to be grandparents."

I try to smile at both of them. Arlen does his best to smile at me, but he keeps casting sidelong glances at his son and then looking away.

Fortunately, the waitress comes by just then, gives us our menus, and we all bend over them. Patricia has to dig around in her purse, find a tissue, and blow her nose before she pulls herself together.

She has to stop herself from looking at Ellis. Her features wrench every time she does.

She concentrates on her menu and I lean over to Ellis. "Do you know what you want? I can order for you if you want me to."

He points at my menu—at the ribs. I burst into a smirk and put my menu down. "You're bad!" I murmur.

He looks away, but I see the corners of his lips twitching. He has to fight himself not to smile back.

I become aware of Arlen staring at us. My cheeks burn so I pretend to straighten my cutlery on the table.

Arlen and Patricia take longer to decide. They put their menus down and we have to face each other across the table.

Arlen breaks the uncomfortable silence first. "So.....have you set a date yet?" he asks me.

"We haven't talked about it." I catch myself glancing at Ellis for help. "He just proposed to me last night.....so I guess we haven't ironed out any of the details yet. Did you two have a big wedding?"

"Oh, sure," Arlen tells me. "My family insisted on having a massive event with three hundred guests. My parents went to a huge expense." He puts out his hand to me. "We don't expect you to do it that way. It isn't for everyone. It certainly wasn't for me." He laughs nervously, shoots his eyes toward his wife, and then dissolves the rest of the way into giggles. "I was a nervous wreck in front of all those people. I wouldn't do it that way if I had to do it over—or, I should say that I wouldn't do it that way if my parents gave me any choice about it."

"What would you do if you had to do it over?" I ask.

"I would have something small—something intimate—maybe with just the two immediate families. Most of those people didn't have to be there at all. They didn't even know us."

"Who were they? Why did your parents insist on inviting so many people and making it so much bigger than it had to be?"

"My father invited a whole bunch of people from his personal business network. He wanted to show off and turn our wedding into a status symbol. I found out years later that he had political ambitions and the wedding was his way of kickstarting that, but it never came to anything. He started having health problems and had to dial back his business dealings anyway, so his political aspirations didn't come to anything. When I look back on it now, I think it was a stupid thing to do—putting that kind of pressure on a young couple right when they're starting out—turning them into some kind of spectacle in front of the whole town...."

He trails off, casts one last helpless glance at his wife, and looks down at his plate. "I probably shouldn't be talking like that."

"I really appreciate you saying so," I tell him. "I've never gotten married. I need the guidance of people who have gone through it before."

"Keep it small if you can," he tells me and looks at his wife again. "But maybe Patty feels differently."

"No, I agree." Patricia pulls herself together, throws back her head, shakes her hair out of her eyes, and sets her mouth in a determined line. "You're absolutely right, Jessie dear. You and Ellis should be very happy together and you both deserve all the support you can get from us. I'm really sorry I overreacted. I can't congratulate both of you enough."

"Thank you so much," I tell her. "I can't wait."

She turns to her son. Her eyes well up with tears again when she looks at him, but she doesn't back away.

She extends her arm across the table and squeezes his above his wrist. "I love you, darling. I love you more than anything—and I love you no matter what you do or how you act or how much you talk. I love you as much like this as I loved you any other way. I'm so sorry. I just didn't know how to take it when I first realized. I promise I'll do better and I swear to you that you and Jessie will have my undying support—no matter what."

"Thank you so much," I tell her. "That means so much coming from you."

Ellis looks up at her. His eyes overflow with so much agonizing heartache. I love him for that. He just wants his parents to be proud of him no matter what he does.

She gets out of her chair and gives him a quick hug. He hugs her back before she sits back down and throws down her tissue all businesslike. "Right. Thank goodness all of that is out of the way. Now let's get to work. We have a wedding to plan!"

I find myself giggling. "Yeah!"

"You won't be able to do anything until you set the date," Arlen points out.

"Nonsense!" Patricia counters. "We can start looking at designs for her dress—and the cake—and you can start planning who to invite."

"We'll probably have another firehouse wedding," I remark. "Our closest friends have all gotten married there—and it means our on-duty crewmates can attend. They wouldn't be able to otherwise."

Patricia points at me and then slams her hand down on the table. "Yes! That's perfect! It's the perfect venue. It's big enough and you have kitchen facilities there. Yes! Ellis was telling me about some of the firehouse weddings—I mean he told me before all this happened."

"Of course."

"Do you have a big family, darling?" she asks me. "Who would you like to invite?"

"Just my immediate family and some of my cousins and aunts and uncles—not too many. What about you?"

"Ellis has some cousins and aunts and uncles, too, but they're all old or living in other parts of the country. I can pass the word around and figure out who will be able to come. That will give you a better idea of how many people to invite."

"That's great! Thank you so much for your help."

She beams at me across the table. "This is going to be wonderful. I'm excited."

The waitress comes just then and takes Patricia's and then Arlen's orders. The waitress turns to me next.

"Ellis and I will both have the ribs," I tell her. "With sides of coleslaw, mashed potatoes, and fries for both of us—and two lemonades."

The waitress scribbles on her notepad. She doesn't bat an eyelash that I ordered for both of us.

Arlen and Patricia glance back and forth between us, but in a minute, the waitress gathers up our menus and leaves us to it.

We spend the rest of the time talking about other things. The two parents ask me about the call that ended with Ellis regaining his memory.

"I wasn't there," I tell them. "I was on the opposite side of the scene. There was so much other stuff going on that I didn't even hear the gunshot. I didn't find out about it until after we transported all the patients. Then Duke told me."

"That's terrible!" Arlen exclaims. "The guy must have been out of his mind to pull a gun on emergency workers like that."

"He did have a really bad head injury," I explain. "He couldn't have been thinking clearly."

Ellis stuns all of us by mumbling under his breath. "It was road rage."

We all spin around to stare at him. He keeps his eyes on his plate and won't look up.

"It was?!" I gasp.

He nods at nothing. "Jim Walker told Carter."

I blink at the side of his head. "So.....he had the gun beforehand?"

Ellis nods again. "He caused the wreck by shooting at other cars."

"Wow!" I gasp. "That's awful!"

"Is he being charged with anything?" Arlen asks.

"He must be," I tell him. "Jim Walker is the Chief of Police. The Police must be charging the guy with reckless endangerment and assault with a deadly weapon at a minimum. I'm not sure if all the patients survived, but if they didn't, the guy will be facing homicide charges, too."

Arlen shakes his head. "I don't know how you people can face it going out there every day. I couldn't do it."

I beam at him. "It's the best job ever. None of us would do anything else."

"That's what Ellis always says."

We go back to talking about other stuff and the conversation eventually turns back to the subject of me and Ellis spending the rest of our lives together.

Arlen and Patricia give us tips on what to look for in a house where we plan to raise kids—and then they start reminiscing about raising Ellis and his older brother, Alonso.

Alonso died in a boating accident when he was twenty-two, so Ellis is Arlen and Patricia's only living child.

Both Arlen and Patricia get teary-eyed with laughter when they relate silly stories from Ellis's and Alonso's childhoods.

Then the food comes. I catch Ellis's eyes twinkling at me while we eat our ribs. Ellis doesn't say another word through the whole meal, but I know he's thinking it.

We're going to be okay. We're getting married and nothing will keep us apart.

Chapter 32: Ellis

J essie runs down her checklist and points her pencil at each item. "The flowers and the caterers are showing up at ten to set up the garage for the ceremony to start at noon."

"We already have a permit from the city to put out cones on the street," Duke replies. "We'll isolate enough curb space to park all the vehicles on the street for the ceremony and the reception. We'll need to move the trucks and ambulances out before the florists and caterers get there."

"All the guests should be gone by four," Keith adds. "We can move the vehicles back inside the firehouse then."

Jessie turns to Danny and Josh. All of us sit around Billy's living room talking about the wedding plans—or everyone else talks while I listen.

"You'll need to make sure you get Ellis back to his house by ten o'clock at the latest," Jessie tells Danny. "I don't know what you plan to do with him for the bachelor party. Just bring him back without too much internal or external damage. That's all I ask."

Everybody laughs and I find myself joining in. My cheeks burn. I'm getting married in a few days. These guys are planning my bachelor party.

"You don't have to worry about any internal or external damage," Billy tells her. "It's just us and we're all married. We won't let anything happen to him. It isn't like we're taking him to a strip club or anything."

Caleb pretends to spin around. "We aren't?! What the hell kind of bachelor party is this?! I want my money back!"

More laughter erupts and Danny swats his shoulder. "Settle down, big dog. You're such a prude you didn't even have a bachelor party."

"That's exactly why I have to make up for it now," Caleb counters. "What are we doing if we aren't taking him to a strip club?"

"There are no strip clubs in Howe," Billy points out. "We would have to travel for that and we wouldn't get back in time for the ceremony."

Now it's Brooke's turn to spin around. "How do you know there aren't any strip clubs in Howe?"

Billy turns bright red and looks away in the other direction. "I wasn't always married, you know."

The others laugh some more.

"What we do and where we go for the bachelor party is a closely guarded government secret," Josh announces. "If you aren't involved in the planning, you'll find out the night of the party. We can't risk any womenfolk finding out our plans."

"The government doesn't have anything to do with this, champ," Keith interjects. "They wouldn't touch this one with a ten-foot pole."

Ellen turns to Jessie. "Don't worry. They'll just go to one of the guy's houses, drink and eat way too much, tell a bunch of stupid jokes, and then pass out. I'm sure Ellis will be there in time for the ceremony."

"I'm more concerned that he'll be able to see straight enough to know who he's marrying," Jessie mumbles.

"Half of us have to work the next day," Carter points out. "We won't be able to drink enough to wake up hung over anyway. If it really means that much to you, I promise to keep an eye on him and make sure he doesn't get too shit-faced the night before. I wouldn't want you to marry anyone who wasn't in peak form."

She blushes and smiles at him. "Thanks, Carter. You're a prince."

"Oh, come on!" Josh interjects. "You don't actually think the rest of us are really going to do anything, do you? Ellen is right. This is going to be the tamest bachelor party in history. Hell, we might even break out the yarn and knitting needles for a little light entertainment."

Everyone explodes and people throw handfuls of potato chips at him.

"Hey!" Brooke roars. "I'm the one who has to clean up this house! Pick up your trash, you kindergarteners!"

Everyone is laughing too hard to go on with the conversation for at least five minutes. General conversation breaks out and a few people pick up the scattered food.

They leave plenty of crumbs behind, though. I'm glad we aren't having this meeting at my house.

I can't stop myself from laughing along with them. I look around the circle at all my favorite people.

Leila and Naomi are at home with the two babies and Emily is one month away from giving birth. She couldn't come, but all three of them have been up to their necks in helping Jessie plan the wedding, too.

Everyone else is here. Duke, Keith, Danny, Billy, Brooke, Josh, Chris, Carter, Sophie, Ellen, Caleb, and Allison.

Ellen turns to Jessie. "Did you take what you need back to your apartment so you and Ellis don't see each other for three days before the wedding?"

Jessie turns bright red and bends over her notepad. "Yeah, I'm all ready. Ellis is driving me home tonight. Then we're working opposite shifts tomorrow and the next day. We won't see each other."

"What about at shift changes?" Allison asks. "You might pass each other in the locker room. Isn't that forbidden?"

"I think they can handle passing each other in the locker room without tearing each other's clothes off," Caleb points out.

Everyone laughs. "You might be surprised," Danny teases. "You know what they say about locker rooms."

"Do we need to assign you a chaperon?" Keith asks.

"I'm sure we can get into and out of the locker room without doing anything inappropriate," Jessie mumbles.

"You aren't allowed to talk to each other, either," Chris points out. "You aren't supposed to see each other, so if we're making this the exception, then you can't talk to each other."

"Who are you kidding?" Josh counters. "Ellis wouldn't talk to her anyway even if it wasn't right before the wedding. We don't need to make a rule about that."

The others laugh and I feel my cheeks burning. It makes me so emotional that my friends can joke about my silence. Everyone accepts it. No one considers it anything to worry about. It's just the way I am now.

"Do we have any other relevant business to discuss—emphasis on relevant?" Duke asks. "Some of us have to work tomorrow, remember?"

"I'm done," Jessie replies. "I think we have everything covered."

"Then I declare this meeting adjourned." He stands up. "I gotta go, people. I'll see you all on the flip side."

Everyone yells after him, "Good night, Duke!" on his way out of the house. Keith, Danny, and Ellen leave at the same time.

The others stand around shooting smartass remarks back and forth for a little while. I wander over to Jessie and slip my hand into hers.

She glances up at me and reads my mind. It's time for us to go, too.

We go through the remaining guests, hug and kiss everyone goodbye, and they all wish us good luck in the days ahead.

Jessie and I finally make it outside. The dark silence of night cuts off the noise and light from inside.

I lead Jessie to my pickup, open the passenger door, and hand her into the seat before I drive her across town to her apartment building.

I park outside, switch off the motor, and we both stare through the windshield at the building. Lights shine in all its windows—all except one.

"I never thought I'd come back here," she murmurs. "Now I'm coming back here to get ready for our wedding. I can't believe it!"

I turn to face her and see the same light beaming out of her eyes that I feel breaking my heart in half. Christ, I love her so much!

I lean across the seat to kiss her. She turns to me just as fast, wraps her arms around my neck, and falls into my kiss with all her passionate warmth.

I can't keep away from her. I lift her onto my lap and hold her there while we kiss for the ages. I have to kiss her enough to make up for the missing the next three days.

Three days. After that, I'll be a married man. I'll take her home to our house and we'll stay there forever.

We'll only move when we buy a bigger house—the house where our children will grow up, skin their knees, break their arms when they fall out of trees, and draw on the walls with their crayons.

I can only stand to let her go for the next three days because I know what is waiting for me on the other end. I wouldn't let her go at all if not for that.

Three days. I can wait three days.

She eases back and gazes deep into my eyes with all her mysterious power. Her fingers keep tracing my face and hair. Her body breathes with life in my arms.

"I love you," she whispers. "I love you more than I can stand."

I gaze back into her eyes feeling all this breaking love. My heart isn't big enough to contain it. I don't have the words to express how I feel about her. Love doesn't even begin to cover it.

I don't have to say it because she already knows. She sees in the way I look at her, the way I take her, the way we smile at each other across the breakfast table.

She feels it in the way I hold her while we fall asleep at night.

She contains all the memories of all the places and trials we've gone through and all the dreams of the life we're going to have in the future.

Every kiss and every embrace speaks volumes of the past and the future coming together in this moment.

She leans into me and falls back into my arms. I could hold her here on my lap all night long. I'm not technically supposed to stop seeing her until after tonight. I could theoretically go until sunrise before I drive away.

We both know that won't happen. She finally sits back. It's time. We both know it.

We both want to get this over with so we can get to the wedding and beyond.

Chapter 33: Ellis

Jessie shifts back to her own seat and I get out to open her door for her.

She straightens her clothes and shakes her hair back into place. I take her hand and lead her toward her apartment building.

I stop her at the door, turn her to face me, cradle her beautiful cheeks in my hands, and bring her in to kiss her. Her kisses never tasted so sweet.

We break apart and just stand there with our arms around each other. I couldn't say anything now if my life depended on it. I need her so much. It tears me apart to let her go even for a few days.

I finally straighten up. Every graze of my hands across her back and sides seems to be carved out of time.

She touches my cheek one last time, rises on her tiptoes, and steals one last kiss. "Bye," she whispers.

"Bye," I tell her.

"I love you," she murmurs. "Don't drink too much at the bachelor party, okay?"

I can't stop myself from smiling. I kiss her knuckles and back away toward the parking lot.

I can't turn around, though. I walk backward so I can keep her in sight all the time until she vanishes inside.

I retreat to the truck and stare up at the building until I see the light switch on in the window.

She comes to the window and smiles out at me gazing up at her.

She places her hand against the glass. Her eyes sparkle with so much love and desire. She's beyond beautiful.

She finally blows me a kiss, pulls the curtain, and her shadow moves away from the window. A minute later, the light switches off, but I can't turn away.

I stand there staring up at her window feeling.....I can't even describe the storm of emotions rushing through me.

I feel exhilarated and sad and powerful all at the same time. I could stand out here for three whole days and wait for her to come out and marry me. I would do it if I had to.

I could do it easily with no effort at all. I would do a lot more than that to get her to marry me.

Nothing happens, though. I keep watching, but nothing happens. She doesn't come back. She doesn't turn on the light.

I would stand here watching over her while she sleeps, but I have to work tomorrow, too.

It will be hard enough trying to get through my shift knowing what will happen at the end of the week.

I turn away to get into my truck to drive home. The house won't feel the same without Jessie there, but that's kind of the point, isn't it? It isn't my house anymore. It's our house.

It's our life now. She's more than a part of my life. She's even more than my life.

There is no her and there is no me. There's just us. We're one unit now. We have a house. We have a schedule. We have a plan.

I pull open my door to get behind the wheel, slide into the seat, and bend over to turn the ignition.

I take one last look at her window.....and that's the moment when I notice a different light coming through one of the other windows of the same building.

It's an open window—a dark window—or it should be.

The curtains are open. I can't see any furniture or people inside. The apartment looks deserted—so deserted that I can see straight through the apartment and through another window to a different building behind this one.

I would recognize the flicker of flames anywhere. They lick from the roof of a building in the next block.

The fire doesn't look from here like it's penetrating into the building itself, but I can't be certain.

I throw my truck into gear, burn rubber around the block, and skid into the building parking lot. I don't have time to mess around here. The flames are already spreading down the walls to the top story of apartments.

I take a split second to turn off the motor before I jump out and sprint into the building.

I burst into the lobby, rip the fire alarm lever down, and the alarm starts blaring through the building. I charge over to the apartment manager's door and pound my fist on it while I yank my phone out of my pocket.

I'm already holding the phone to my ear waiting for the 911 dispatcher to answer by the time the building manager comes to the door. People are already pouring out of their apartments and crowding the stairs.

The manager is an old black man in his boxer shorts and a wife-beater tank top. He squints at me. "What the hell....?"

"The roof is on fire!" I yell at him over all the noise. "Get everyone out of the building! I'm calling the Fire Department!"

"911 emergency dispatch," a female operator chirps in my ear. "Please state the nature of the emergency."

"There's a building on fire at the corner of Chamberlain Avenue and Park Place!" I yell into the phone. "This is Ellis Barrett from the Howe County Fire Department! I'm already evacuating the building. The fire is isolated on the roof at the moment. I'm going in to make sure everyone gets out on the top floor! We need fire and possibly ambulance crews on scene immediately!"

"Yes, Sir," the dispatcher tells me. "I'm dispatching them now."

I can't wait any longer. I make sure the manager is putting on his bathrobe and coming out to deal with all the evacuating tenants.

I take off for the stairs, but I have a hard time getting up them with so many people coming down from above.

I keep the phone glued to my ear until I hear the operator tell me that the fire crew is on the way. Good.

I hang up and finally get to the stairs above the evacuating crowd. If anyone is trapped up here, they won't be able to get out.

I make it to the top landing to find the flames already invading from the roof. I jump down to the top story of apartments, burst through the door, and go from one apartment to another.

The tenants evacuated so fast that half of them left their doors standing open. The few that are closed are all unlocked. Everyone was too concerned with getting out.

I stick my head into each apartment. "Is anyone in here?!" I roar. "The building is on fire! I'm with the Fire Department! Call out if you can hear me!"

No one answers until I come to the last apartment. The door is shut. It's one of the few that is and it's locked. Someone must be trapped inside.

I take a step back and kick the door in. "Is anyone here!" I barge into the living room.....and stop in my tracks.

An oxygen tank, nebulizer, and a stack of medications sits next to the living room recliner. I have seen these way too many times not to recognize the signs.

"I'm with the Fire Department!" I yell into the first room. "We need to evacuate the building!"

I get to the last bedroom. An even bigger oxygen tank stands by the bed.

An old man struggles to sit up, but his arms and legs are so frail that he can't even prop himself on his elbow.

An oxygen cannula runs from his nose to the giant tank standing by the bed. He's too old, weak, and sick to get out of bed, much less evacuate the building.

I don't even think about it. I rush him and pull a blanket around his shoulders. "Stay here, Sir. I'm going to get you out."

"Help me...." he chokes. "Please..."

"Don't worry, Sir," I tell him. "I got you. Don't worry."

My heart threatens to explode when I bolt back to the living room. Flames lick around the windows. I need to work fast before the fire gets near these oxygen tanks—especially the big one.

I take the smaller tank into the bedroom, transfer his cannula tubing to the small tank, and then pick up the old man.

I wrap the blanket around him, but I don't dare to carry him over my shoulder. I might break him in half. He wouldn't be able to breathe in that position anyway.

I put the tank between his legs and scoop up the whole package in my arms. He keeps whimpering in terrified helplessness when I angle him out of the apartment and set off for the stairs.

They're deserted now, thank Heaven. He weighs nothing, but I have to consciously slow myself down so I don't miss my footing.

"Thank you, son," he wheezes on our way down.

"Sit tight, Sir," I pant. "The ambulances will check you over when we get down to the street."

I make it to the tenth floor before I meet the crew coming back up. "Is anyone else up there?" Keith asks me.

"I checked the top floor," I gasp. "I didn't get a chance to check anywhere else."

He pats me on the back and pushes me down the stairs behind the crew as they continue the rest of the way up. This fire isn't my problem anymore.

I'm panting hard by the time I get outside and hand over the old man to Chris and Brooke on the ambulance. I can barely breathe well enough to give them my report.

The old man is fine, though—apart from whatever was wrong with him to begin with.

I buckle onto the ambulance step and rest my elbows on my knees while I catch my breath. Duke comes over to me and grips my shoulder. "You okay?"

I nod. I'm breathing too heavily to say anything, but there's nothing to say anyway. It's over. The fire crew will handle it from here.

I hear Brooke talking to the old man behind me. The paramedics hook him up to the ambulance oxygen supply and she takes his medical history.

I straighten up to look around. I'm exhausted, but I still don't feel right about sitting here doing nothing while the crew works all around me.

I stand up.....and freeze for the second time when I notice the wind blowing the fire toward the next building. It's heading straight for Jessie's building.

Chapter 34: Jessie

I wake up from a sound sleep when someone shakes me gently by the shoulder. "Jessie—wake up! You have to wake up, Jessie!"

I flounder out of my daze and realize that Ellis is standing over me. "Huh?" I try to look around.

It takes me a minute to remember that I'm in my old apartment. I'm not sleeping in the bedroom I share with Ellis.

The whole thing comes rushing back. The meeting....the wedding......We aren't supposed to see each other before the wedding.

He doesn't give me a chance to ask. "You have to get out of the building right away," he murmurs under his breath. "The building next door is on fire and the wind is blowing the flames this way. Come on. Get up. We're evacuating the building."

He pulls me to my feet before I fully comprehend what he's saying. He grabs my bathrobe from the dresser.

My duffel bag with all my stuff in it still sits there. Everything I brought with me for the next three days is in that bag. I've already moved everything else I own out of this apartment.

Ellis doesn't wait for my brain to kick back into gear. He wraps the robe around me and steers me out of the apartment. He doesn't even give me a chance to blink the sleep out of my eyes.

We walk out into a scene of mass evacuation. Police officers go from one apartment to another waking everybody up, steering everyone toward the stairs, stopping people from grabbing their belongings, and then going through every apartment one room at a time to make sure they don't miss anyone.

Ellis wraps his arm around my shoulders and holds me tight against his body. He doesn't let go of me once all the way downstairs.

The tenants crowd into the parking lot. The fire crew is all over there working on the building next door.

A crane stands between the two buildings with a massive jet of water spouting from the crane basket onto the other building's roof.

Ellis stays with me for a long time until the fire crew gets the other building under control.

I spot Duke having a conversation with the surrounding Police officers. They come back to our group. "You can all go back inside. The Fire Chief is giving this building the all-clear. It's safe for you all to return to your apartments."

Ellis turns to me. "I have to go help the crew."

I grab his hand. "Let me come with you."

He glances over his shoulder toward the fire trucks and ambulances in the distance.

"Does anyone over there need medical treatment?" I ask. "Do they need another paramedic?"

He doesn't answer. He takes my hand and we head over to the other parking lot.

He takes me to an ambulance with an old man lying on the gurney. Brooke sits on the bench filling out her paperwork while Chris checks a little boy's eyes, ears, and mouth on the ambulance's back step.

Ellis takes off to go help the guys finish dealing with the burning building.

"Do you need any help?" I ask Chris. "Do any other patients need transport?"

"No one needs transport," Brooke tells me. "Unless you count this old gentleman and he isn't critical."

I eye the patient. "What's wrong with him?"

"Apart from everything? He's old and Ellis says he had a bunch of medical equipment and medications in his apartment. Now he has nowhere else to spend the night. We're taking him to the hospital until his relatives can arrange another place for him."

"What do you mean—Ellis says he had a bunch of medical equipment?"

Brooke looks up at me. "Ellis was the one who raised the alarm about the fire. He pulled the alarm to evacuate the building. He called 911 and then he went through the top floor to make sure everyone got out. He rescued this man from his apartment because the patient couldn't walk on his own." She gives me a soft, sad smile. "You really are marrying a hero, sweetie."

I catch Chris looking at me the same way. "Ellis was also the one who noticed the flames heading for your building. He raised the alarm and got the Police there in time to evacuate everyone."

I blink at my two friends in shock. Ellis.....he saved the day again.

I turn around very slowly. He works as energetically as ever to help the guys roll up their hoses, load all their gear onto the trucks, and clean up the scene. The fire is out, but not before it leaves the top half of the building charred and partially caved in.

That old man would have been dead for sure if Ellis hadn't gotten to him in time. Heaven only knows how many other people would have died in that building if Ellis hadn't raised the alarm—and in my building.

I can only stand and watch him in amazement. He doesn't hesitate to pitch in wherever the crew needs him. I even hear him laughing at their jokes.

He's come so far in just a few short months. I never expected that he could bounce back from all the disasters that have plagued him.

He's the best man I could ever hope to marry. I just have to get through the next three days.

I want to take him home and jump him right now. I want to shower him with love and kisses. I want to take him to bed and show him how much I want him.

He holds a hasty conversation with Keith, Duke, and Danny before Ellis goes around the building to do something else on the other side.

I'm still standing there when Keith, Duke, and Danny come over to me. "You can go back to your apartment now, sweetie," Keith tells me. "You aren't supposed to see Ellis again until the wedding. You don't need to hang around here anymore."

Danny smirks at me. "You broke that rule already, so there will be severe punishments on the wedding night."

I find myself blushing. Keith glares at his brother and then at me. "We're calling this an exceptional circumstance, so we're letting you off easy this once. You don't need to hang around anymore, though. We got it covered on this end. We'll make sure Ellis gets home in one piece." He points toward my building. "Go on. Go back to bed."

I blink at them and then grin at all of them. "Thanks, guys." I rush them and hug each of them one after the other.

Keith chuckles and pushes me away. "Quit stalling. You're as bad as he is. You won't leave an emergency scene alone, will you?"

I hug Brooke and Chris, too, but Keith is right. I'm not accomplishing anything here except losing sleep.

I cast one last look toward the rescue truck. Ellis isn't there any-more—or if he is, the crew is keeping him out of my sight. Damn it. This crew is just too conscientious.

I heave an almighty sigh. I can't stay here any longer.

Danny steps forward and holds out his hand. "Come on, sweet-heart. I'll walk you home."

"You dog!" Chris yells after him. "Moving in on the bride?!"

"She's perfectly safe with me. I'm sure the groom trusts me with Jessie's virtue."

The two girls howl with laughter as Danny leads me away.

He takes me into the building and back to my apartment, but I hesitate to go inside. I want Ellis. I want him really bad.

"Are you gonna be okay?" Danny asks.

"Yeah....I just....." I keep looking around at nothing. I'm the only tenant still outside their apartment. "I just really wish I could see him again."

"He's a hero. He's out there flying around in his cape saving air-planes from crashing out of the sky and stopping the nuclear apoca-lypse."

I snort with laughter. "No, he isn't."

"You're right, but he is pretty freakin' great. You got yourself a good one." He kisses me on the forehead. "Now go to sleep. I'll see you tomorrow morning."

He waits until I go inside and shut the door. Now I really have no excuse not to do as he says.

I go into my room and sit down on the bed. It seems like only a few minutes since I did this before.

I looked down from my apartment window at Ellis standing by his truck. He gazed back up at me....and I blew him a kiss.

Waiting three days until I see him again just got astronomically harder. I really want to hold him.....and kiss him.....and envelop him in all the love in my heart.....

That will have to wait.

I lie down in bed, but I stay awake for hours thinking about him. He must have talked a lot tonight—maybe the most he's ever talked since John's death.

I've never been prouder of him. I've never been prouder to call him mine.

I'm going to marry this man if it's the last thing I do. I'll never let him go.

I'm going to make him the happiest man alive just as soon as we get to the altar and tie the knot.

Chapter 35: Ellis

I check my appearance in the mirror, smooth down the jacket of my tux, and for no reason, I burst into nervous laughter. I'm about to get married. Jesus, I can't believe it!

"Is something wrong?" Keith asks behind me. "Did you suddenly grow a Rudolf the Red-nosed Reindeer nose in the last five minutes?"

I turn away from the mirror. I've already checked my appearance a thousand times.

If I don't look good enough by now, looking again and straightening my jacket and cuffs won't help.

I have to work hard not to bite back a stupid grin. The excitement is starting to get to me.

Okay, that's wrong. The excitement already got to me a long time ago. I'm about to see Jessie in a few minutes.

Keith, Danny, Josh, Carter, and Caleb crowd my living room. They all wear matching grey tuxes with black bow ties. The guys all look outstanding, of course. I just hope I look half as outstanding as they do.

I know I look pretty good. I just hope I'm good enough for Jessie—but I already know that, too.

I get another rush of nervous excitement when I think about seeing her. I don't even know what her wedding dress looks like. The women have been over-the-top secretive about all the details.

My mom has been heavily involved with all the firehouse wives in planning everything for the wedding. I don't even want to know half of what they've been talking about behind my back.

Ellen turned out to be right about the so-called bachelor party. We had it at Caleb's house since it's the biggest.

All we did was stand around, talk, eat, drink a little bit, and hang out. We all quit early and everyone went home. It was hardly even a party, but it was exactly what I needed.

None of the guys even talked about their wives or their marriages. I would have felt really uncomfortable if they did.

They mostly just talked about firehouse business. Duke and Keith talked about Leon and Amelia.

Danny talked to Keith about Oakleigh and the problems she's been having since John's death.

Danny also talked to Keith and Duke about Emily's pregnancy, but they kept it low-key. Josh listened in, now that Chris is pregnant, too.

I stayed on the outside listening in. All these married men were the perfect company for me the night before my wedding.

I don't have to wonder what married life will be like. I just have to look around me to see the evidence right in front of my eyes.

I don't even want to go out to a bar or a strip club. I don't want or need to see what I'm missing. I don't miss being single at all. I just want to go home to Jessie and forget about all of that.

These men around me right now—they're all so good for me. They surround me in so much comradely love and admiration.

They support me. They know I'm going to be a good husband and father exactly like they are.

I love each of them for that. I can tell when they look at me that they love me, too. They admire me and respect me for the work I do—and for the person I am.

I have nothing to prove to them because I already have proved it a dozen times over. I'm as much a part of them as they are of me.

Keith comes over to me, squares his shoulders in front of me, and pretends to scowl at me under his heavy eyebrows.

He straightens my jacket lapels even though they're fine. "You look really good," he tells me. "You look good enough to get married."

My cheeks burn and I lower my eyes. My throat hurts too much to tell him how grateful I am for his support.

He grips both my shoulders. "You're gonna do just fine, brother," he rumbles. "You are gonna make that little lady very happy."

I look up and see his eyes shining with bottomless love and approval. I have to believe it when he says those words.

He claps me on both shoulders and glances at his watch. "We better get going. Come on."

I keep breaking into nervous laughter on my way out to the car. It's a big Suburban limousine big enough to carry all of us without rumpling our clothes.

I feel like I'm getting away with something I shouldn't. I'm about to marry Jessie. How the hell did I get so lucky?

I keep waiting for someone to come along and bust me and tell me that it's all a bad dream or a giant mistake—but it isn't.

We ride to the firehouse to find the place all set up for the wedding. Most of the guests are already there and sitting in the chairs lined up inside the empty garage.

The two trucks and two ambulances sit parked at the curb in case the on-duty crew gets a call. They wait around in their uniforms. The rest of the off-duty crew that isn't in the wedding party mingles with the other guests.

My mom comes over to me and the guys as soon as we get out of the limo. She kisses me with tears in her eyes. "You look so handsome! I love you so much! This is such a blessed day!"

I wish I could tell her not to make a fuss over me, but she breaks off right away and turns to the other guys.

She goes through the group fitting corsages into our buttonholes and then hustles us to the front of the seats.

The flower arch stands on the other side of the garage with the red carpet passing between the chairs. My mom makes an enormous deal about positioning me in exactly the right place with Keith, Danny, Josh, Carter, and Caleb standing behind me.

She beams at all of us with so much happiness. I can't bring myself to tell her to stop. She's almost as happy about this wedding as I am.

I get another stomach full of butterflies when Duke comes downstairs also dressed in his tux. Jessie is upstairs getting ready. She'll come down in a few minutes.

I can't stop laughing to save my life. Keith saves the day by gripping both my shoulders from behind to shake out my nerves.

I wish I could turn around and look at him and my five groomsmen one last time. I need to see them to bolster my courage to get through this.

I don't have time to turn around before the speakers on the sound system start playing the bridal march.

My knees get weak when Brooke, Chris, and Sophie come downstairs in their bridesmaids' dresses.

My heart stops when I see Jessie. She wears a dress so puffed up with gauze and taffeta that it forms a cloud around her petite frame.

Her actual dress—the part around her body—glistens with shimmering lights of sequins and what look like diamonds. Her body nestles in the center of the cloud like the jewel in the center of a crown of dreams.

I can't stop staring at her as her father walks her down the aisle. She smiles, but she only smiles at me. Her eyes shine only for me. She doesn't see anything but me.

All my nerves evaporate when I see her coming toward me. My whole being goes deadly calm. This is the moment of my destiny—the moment when my life starts making sense.

I hear Duke talking in the background. He gives a short introductory speech and then starts asking Jessie if she takes me as her lawfully wedded husband, in sickness and in health, for better or for worse, and all the other times.

In sickness and in health. For better or for worse. She already has proved that she's there for me in sickness and in health, for better or for worse.

Nothing will ever break us apart. I know that now. We can face any challenge after what we've already gone through.

She says, "I do," and Duke starts asking me the same questions. My lawfully wedded wife. In sickness and in health. For better or for worse. For richer or for poorer. All the days of my life. Hell yes.

I don't take my eyes off her through it all. "I do," I tell her.

She smiles up at me with the same steady determination. She doesn't feel giddy or nervous or excited, either. We both know exactly what this means and what we're doing.

My mind snaps into perfect crystal clarity when Duke says, "I now pronounce you husband and wife. You may kiss the bride."

I scoop her up with both arms behind her back, lift her off the floor, and kiss her madly in front of everyone. I don't care that the whole crew and both our families are watching.

She kisses me back just as hard. Her veil falls over my face. I don't want to let her go or put her down.

Cheers interrupt around us and I eventually have to. She blushes and laughs when I look into her eyes....and then we turn to the guests.

The crew surrounds us, hugs us, congratulates us, and then everyone migrates over to the buffet table for the reception.

I can't stop laughing and smiling at my crewmates. The glow on their faces makes it all worth it. I've never seen them so happy—and I've never been so happy.

That rush of joy vibrates back and forth between all of us. My crewmates tease me, jostle me, hug me, and some of the paramedics even kiss me on the cheek.

My mom puts her arms around me with tears of joy streaming down her cheeks and then hugs Jessie. My mom is so overwrought that she can't even speak.

My dad blinks back tears, too. He has trouble controlling his mouth, but as the hours pass, food and drink flows, we cut the cake, and everyone settles down to just having a good time.

I hold Jessie's hand through it all. Her eyes shine with so much warmth every time I look at her. I never want to stop looking at her.

The time finally comes for her to throw her bouquet and for us to go out to the limo that will take us back to our house.

Our honeymoon will be spent working at the firehouse. Duke can't afford for us to leave. He's already shorthanded enough.

That's okay because I don't want to be anywhere else but right here. I don't want a single day to stand between me and the rest of forever that I'm going to spend with the woman of my dreams.

<u>End of Book 9.</u>

Keep Reading

F<u>irehouse Blues Series: Book 10: Second Chance</u>

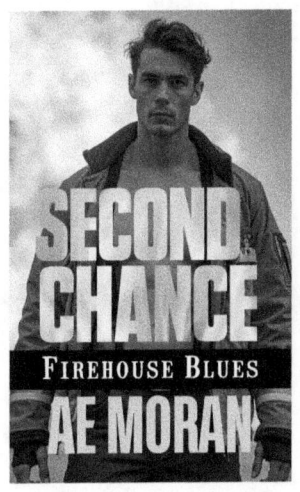

Fire Chief Duke Broebeck has everything he ever dreamed off—a beautiful wife, a precious baby daughter, and another one on the way. Life couldn't get any better—until a deadly car accident costs him everything.

When disaster strikes Howe Firehouse again, only one person can help Duke—paramedic Ellen Foreman Brewer—former FireChief

John Brewer's widow. She doesn't work for Duke the way the rest of the crew does, so she's the only person who can truly be there for him.

Not everyone is happy about the growing bond between these two injured souls. When what starts off as caring and compassion for Duke's tragedy turns to more, the result could derail everything the fire crew has worked to build since John's death. Can the firehouse family survive another devastating blow or will this be the straw that finally tears Howe Firehouse apart?

You can find it at your favorite book retailer.

Get All of AE Moran's Free Books

S ign Up Once—Get all A.E. Moran's free books including brand new releases

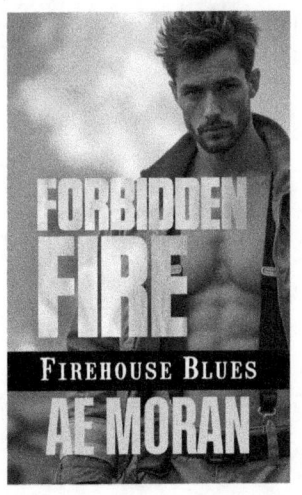

When what you want most is the one thing you can never have......

Austin McAuliffe is every woman's dream firefighter—young, strong, drop-dead hot, and selflessly dedicated to his career—and to the woman of his heart, Emma Brady. Only one other person holds a place in Austin's life—his best friend and fellow firefighter, Theo Gough. Austin insists on Theo spending time with Austin and Emma as a couple, especially when these two firefighters have a hard day at the office.

No one can believe when Austin completely flips out and randomly accuses Theo and Emma of flirting with each other in front of the whole fire crew. Could there be some deeper, more sinister reason for Austin to suddenly lose his mind and lash out at those closest to him?

Emma is devastated when Austin coldly dumps her with no warning and disappears out of her life, but Austin casts a long shadow. The nightmare of his sudden betrayal will come back to haunt Emma and Theo long after Austin is gone. Will the ghosts of the past ruin any chance for them to regain their happiness.....or will Austin's madness take down everyone he cares about along with him?

Sign up at www.authoraemoran.com to read it for free.

About AE Moran

A.E Moran is the contemporary romance pen name for Theo Mann.

I write 70 books per year—and yes, before you ask, all these books are my original creative work. Nothing written under my name is AI-generated or ghostwritten because I write better than AI and any ghostwriter out there.

People don't read fiction for entertainment or to escape from reality. People read fiction to see their humanity reflected in another person's character and story.

This is my promise to you. When you read my books, you'll see your own humanity reflected in the characters and stories. I take this commitment to my readers very seriously. My books are an intimate form of communication between us. I would never disrespect my readers by turning that over to a machine or another writer. This is my bond between me and you as my reader.

I write 20,000 words per day as my daily work output. If anyone with a public platform would like to challenge me to prove this in a controlled environment, feel free to contact me on this website's contact page.

I worked as a professional ghostwriter for fifteen years. Now I'm going for the Guinness World Record by writing 700 books over the next ten years and 1400 books over the next twenty years, all originally written by me. See my website for the full book list.

I'm also the author of *Proof for the Existence of God* and the *Crimes Against Fiction* blog. You can find all my nonfiction work at www.cr imes-against-fiction.com.

If you have a story idea, or if you would like me to explore a series in more depth, or if you'd like me to explore a character by writing a spinoff series about that character or world, leave me a message on my website's contact page. I answer all reader emails, so ask me anything, tell me what you liked and didn't like, and let me know where you'd like your favorite series to go. I would love to hear your ideas and find out what you'd like to read next.

You can find out more at www.theomann.com or at www.author aemoran.com.

Also by AE Moran (so far)

Standalone Novels

Heart on a Knife Edge

Dream Dimension

Just Friends

Back From the Dead

Damaged

Small Town Reunion

Series

Firehouse Blues (Books 1-10)

Turning Point Ranch (Books 1-10)

The Billionaires' Club (Books 1-10)

Paradise Cruises (Book 1-8)

Royal House (1-10)

Summerton Estates (1-10)

www.ingramcontent.com/pod-product-compliance
Lightning Source LLC
Chambersburg PA
CBHW052026020726
47501CB00004B/1263